Days Pass like a Shadow

Days Pass like a Shadow

Paula R. C. Readman

Bridge House

British Library Cataloguing in Publication Data
A Record of this Publication is available from the British
Library

ISBN 978-1-907335-80-8

This edition published 2020 by Bridge House Publishing
Manchester, England

Contents

The Meetings

As I sit on a park bench I trace the words engraved on the small metal plaque with my fingertips. By doing this simple act I recall the happiness I witnessed so long ago.

Every day I come here to watch others enjoying the park. As I sit, I reflect on an unknown person who was once so strong and so full of life, all those years ago. Maybe the plaque could be a marker for my life too. As crazy as it may seem, I used to watch him and her, while I was busy working among the flowerbeds and borders.

Most mornings the young woman would arrive via the side road into the park. Bohemian in her dress she walked briskly, her long, blonde hair streaming out behind her, like a veil of sunshine even on the dullest of days. Her footfall on the gravel was so light it barely made a sound. If I happened to be busy either weeding, hoeing or planting I would miss her arrival.

Sometimes while I straightened my back I would catch sight of her waiting patiently at this bench. On seeing the unknown man's arrival, her face would brighten and with a laugh she would rush to his open arms. The man, tall and elegant in his posture, dressed quite casually in chino trousers and a light jacket. Some mornings he would arrive so early that the mist hadn't time to clear to wait for her. He always came via the main entrance, with its large ornate gates of black and gold. A couple of hours later she would arrive with her beautiful smile.

I never quite knew what time of day they would arrive. Sometimes if the weather was awful in the morning they came in the afternoon, but I never saw them arrive together.

At first, I wasn't sure about their relationship, whether they were lovers, or not? Not that it was any of my business. I just saw them as two happy people enjoying each other's company.

Happiness is a rare thing these days. I considered myself lucky a silent witness to the pleasure they shared as I worked among the flowerbeds and borders. Not being a good judge of age I did think the man looked slightly older than the woman. The sun highlighted the passing of his years in the changing colour of his hair. However, in all honesty, I couldn't begin to guess the woman's age, as I hadn't seen her close up, well, not at first.

I used to see them strolling, arm in arm around the park. The woman gazed into the man's face as though she'd never tire of it. Occasionally, I would stumble across them standing close together down by the fountain, or up on the rise overlooking the town.

He stood with his arm around her narrow waist, talking in his easy, gentle way while pointing out something of interest to her. Like the multitude of colourful butterflies that fed restlessly on the globe buddleia bush. Sometimes, as if by magic, the man would produce a bag of bread. The young woman's laughter carried on the air across to where I was working among the perennials. Together like children they would race along the path to the pond. Her gentle, laughing voice was conveyed on the light summer breeze as she called back to him.

"I win again!"

At the pond, the swans were the first to know there was food on offer. They would haughtily swim over as the woman attempted to throw the bread to them, but the smaller, more agile, comical ducks would get in first. Together the couple would laugh at the antics of the swans and ducks until all the bread had gone.

Some days while I trundled about with my wheelbarrow I would come across them, sitting with their heads intimately close. They were especially fond of the bench under the spreading oak tree on a rise overlooking the town.

On one occasion while I dug out a flowerbed ready for the seasons planting I watched as the man produced a bag of nuts. Within minutes as though by some sixth sense, from nowhere, squirrels appeared and came down from the branches above to feed on the nuts the woman held out.

The unexpected look of pure pleasure that crossed her face was a remarkable sight. It seemed to me the man brought a sort of enchantment into her life. I know he did mine, and I began to look forward to their visits, to share in the magic of their happiness.

It makes me smile even now. I remember sharing her birthdays and Christmas celebrations on this bench. The gentleman was like a magician conjuring brightly coloured balloons and ribbons out of nowhere to decorate the bench before she arrived.

As she came up the rise towards him, he produced a cake with lighted candles. Once she was seated, he'd arrange her flowing bohemian skirt around her sandaled feet and then set up his camera to take a photograph of them together while she blew out the candles.

The autumn seemed to arrive quite quickly that year. You could smell the changing of the seasons in the air. I had only just unlocked the park gates when he appeared out of the early morning mist.

He walked much slower, unsteady on his feet and with the aid of a stick. He seemed embarrassed to see me and nodded his acknowledgement before making a slow progress up the slight rise to wait as he always did on their bench under the oak tree. Shocked at the sudden change in his appearance I quickly turned my attention back to raking the first of the falling leaves. Their absence from the park went unnoticed by me, I'm sorry to say, with too many jobs needing my attention.

As the flowering season ended I began cutting back shrubs, digging out the annuals, dead heading the roses and splitting some of the large plants to make new ones. As I worked my way through the list of jobs my mind was already planning next season's planting. The weeks flew by as I continued working my way around the park, tidying the edge of the pond and pulling out the invasive weeds. Soon I was clearing the flowerbeds, borders and urns ready to plant up with the winter flowering plants and bulbs.

Early one morning I woke to find the first snowfall of the season had fallen overnight. After I had bought a pint of milk I hurried to the park as the snow began to fall again. As I turned the corner, on reaching the shelter of the park keeper's hut, I found the young woman sitting huddled in her coat outside the hut door.

On seeing me she rose. Tears stained her face. With a weak smile she greeted me like an old friend and held out a small, brightly wrapped parcel. Words tumbled from her lips in-between uncontrollable sobs. All I could understand was that she was trying to explain something.

"Please, come in and have a cup of tea. While you warm up you can explain."

On unlocking the door the warmth of the hut hit us, adding colour to her cheeks and hands. I gestured for her to sit on an old park bench I had just finished repairing. While we waited for the kettle to boil she repeated what she had said outside. As I passed her a mug of tea I noticed the fine lines around her eyes.

After taking a sip, she said, "I've been unable to face coming here, to our special place, since the funeral two months ago." Tears bubbled up in her brown eyes as she picked up the parcel and handed it to me.

On opening it I was unable to speak after reading what was written on the plaque in my hands. I met her eyes and she smiled at the shock that must have registered on my face.

"Yes," she said with a rueful laugh. "He was my father. I was only able to search for him after my mother passed away. On our first meeting my father promised me we would do all the things we had missed doing when I was a child. So we flew kites, visited the zoo and built sandcastles on the beach, but mostly we enjoyed spending our time here in the park. I recalled coming here with him as a small child before my parents divorced and my mother took me away. My father had remarried, but unfortunately, they were unable to have children. He kept me a secret from his new wife only wishing to protect her from any upset that might have arisen from our meetings." She took another sip before continuing.

"Three months ago I received a call from Dad's wife to say he'd been rushed into hospital. As his health was deteriorating fast he'd told her all about me. She phoned to ask me to keep her company at his bedside, wanting to share his last moments together. We've since become good friends and I spend my time visiting her now. I would like to have a reminder in the park of the wonderful times I've spent with my lost father and to remind other people of their fathers too. If it's possible could we fit the plaque to the bench under the tree?"

I nodded picking up my screwdriver. Together we stepped out in the snow making our way to the rise. As the young woman held the plaque I fastened the last screw in place before she read the words aloud:

"In memory of all the lost fathers everywhere: One day may your children come back into your lives so you can relive their childhood years together again."

As I watched her leave by the main gates I recall the happy times I spent with my father playing on my sledge on sunny wintry days so long ago. As I made my way back to my hut I saw our footprints were the only ones in the freshly fallen snow and wondered whether I would see her again.

Burning the Midnight Oil

It felt odd being the only mourner at the crematorium, listening to what the vicar had to say about my mother; after all, they were things I already knew. My mind began to wander as I thought about all the people who could've joined me in celebrating her life.

Suddenly a door banged at the back of the crematorium disrupting my thoughts. Propriety stopped me from turning to see who were arriving late, though in all honesty, I wasn't expecting anyone else.

Oh dear God I'm finding it hard to get used to the fact it's no longer *we* but *me* now. I can't remember a time in my twenty-four years when it wasn't *us* – her and me. The reality of her leaving hits me again. I glanced at her photo perched on the coffin for reassurance. The pain in my heart made me want to shout, 'why now?' Just the thought of her heading off on a journey alone crushes me.

I tried to focus on what the vicar was saying just in case the door banging was Mother storming out in frustration at being kept waiting. It wouldn't have surprised me if it was her. If we were waiting for a taxi she would have her shoes and coat on ready long before it was due to arrive.

As the vicar paused to take a breath I glanced over my shoulder. I couldn't see anyone behind and guessed it must've been one of the undertakers leaving. I had hoped some of the neighbours might've seen the announcement in the paper and joined me, though we were only really on nodding terms with most of them.

Mother was outspoken which put most people off getting to know her. She had a habit of keeping herself to herself. She especially despised time-wasters or people who couldn't be bothered to do things properly. She spoke more to the postman, and the man in the corner shop, but I wasn't really expecting them. The service was at their busiest time of the day. I looked up and saw the vicar had his head bowed in prayer, so I lowered mine, and mumbled along. My thoughts were still racing.

Somehow it didn't seem right her dying. Of course, I understand life eventually reaches it natural conclusion. We all have to leave in the end. It's just that her life seemed so unfulfilled. Maybe she would've been a different person, if she had experienced more love in her life. I don't suppose it helped with Father leaving us when I was a baby.

As the curtains closed around the coffin the vicar intoned the final blessing. It felt more to me like the curtains coming down on the last matinee of an unsuccessful theatre show. Goodness knows Mother and I had seen plenty of them. She often remarked while we were catching the last bus home after an evening out at the theatre. "Once again Harold, we've wasted good money on rubbish. I've no idea what that play was all about?"

So many times I'd wanted to share my thoughts with her on the plays we'd seen, but I learned quite quickly that she wasn't interested in my views. She always added as an afterthought, "Well, at least we had a lovely time together. If anything it's a reason to get our glad rags on."

From the crematorium I headed towards the park wanting to give myself headspace. For months we'd known she had an inoperable cancer. While I spent the time trying to come to terms with her leaving, she'd spent it planning her own funeral. Mother wasn't one for trusting others.

As good days rolled into bad ones I sat in her bedroom while she thumbed through her record collection, choosing music, hymns, and prayers. It felt we were planning a surprise party but all too soon her face portrayed the changes the illness was making.

On Mother's good days I often arrived home from work to find her in the kitchen cooking. "I get so bored doing nothing all day." Her face flushed from the heat of the oven. "I had to do something so I cooked dinner for you."

One afternoon I arrived home to a cold, empty kitchen. I knocked on her bedroom door. The voice from within was incoherent. I found her sitting up in bed, pale and thin, so unlike Mother. Her sunken, watery eyes closed, while her bird-like hands rested on a large brown envelope in her lap.

In my entire life she had always been up, dressed and busy, never one for taking to her bed during the day. Mother had never been a big woman. Her hair once dark brown, now hung like a drab, faded curtain around her bony shoulders as she sat so still, half the person, she used to be.

Nervously I'd reached out, touching her. Unable to believe she had left me so soon. She'd been so cold to the touch that I'd sunk to my knees.

"Oh Mum," I whispered, my heart breaking.

She gave a sudden cough. Relief flooded through me. She patted my head and croaked, "I haven't gone yet."

I lifted the envelope from her, setting it down on the bedside cabinet.

"Don't open…" she said, her voice barely a whisper.

"I won't. Can I get you anything?"

She shook her head, "Nothing at the moment. Is there any post?"

"None. Are you waiting for something?"

"I'm tired." I moved the pillows that propped her up and helped her to lie down. "See you in the morning. I promise," she said, with a tiny smile.

Three weeks later, she left me – she was icy cold to the touch. On rediscovering the envelope Mother had been clutching a few days before she died I found it contained a to-do-list and all the phone numbers I needed. Even at the end of her life she still felt I wasn't capable of doing what needed to be done. It's not that I hadn't thought about leaving home before and making a life for myself. I had many times, but somehow it felt I was betraying her, in the same way as Father had when he left.

Once we knew her time was running out, I had begun to make lists of possibilities as my freedom loomed on the horizon. To my dismay, I discovered within the excitement of planning my new future traces of guilt which robbed me of the pleasure, knowing she was about to leave forever.

Arriving at the park I followed the path, and caught glimpses of our home between the tall trees. Dark, Gothic, and menacing in the waning afternoon light with its fading Victorian grandeur. I pushed open the gate, and stood in the garden staring up. The top floor windows stared down like soulless cat's eyes, double-lidded with grubby net curtains, some torn in places hung limply alongside cobwebs, as years of neglect dulled the once shiny glass. Maybe we should have sold the house years ago. Being so large it would have been converted into luxury apartments for the wealthy by now. Mother's once prized garden would've disappeared under concrete to support the ever-growing numbers of cars filling the roads around the park.

On entering the cold kitchen, I recalled how for years, nothing seemed to change. In the past whenever I came home from school I would find Mother standing before the range cooking, the house warm, cosy, and homely. Years later, still the same when I finished a working day. Mother would be in the kitchen ready to dish up my dinner, hers already eaten.

"Why didn't you wait?" I would have asked her.

"I got hungry," was her reply.

I wanted her to share a meal other than just Christmas

dinner, or on my birthday. Mother looked after everything, so there was nothing for me to worry about when I asked to take on some of the responsibility she would say, "No different to having a wife,"

I wanted to point out there was one big difference. I hoped to God she was wrong for having a wife meant sex. I suppose Mother must have tried sex at least once. Maybe she found it wasn't for her? I could imagine her saying to Father, "No, thank you. Never, never again." Maybe that's why he left her; it wasn't to his liking, a sexless marriage. She's never really spoken about Father, apart from the fact that he worked abroad. Of course, I've tried asking. I would approach the subject carefully. She never liked too many questions at once.

"You're confusing me. Why do you want to know that? Can't a woman have secrets of her own? Bet you've got a few of your own, Har… old?"

She had a way of stretching my name out, making it sound sordid. As soon as she did that, I knew I had to change the subject. I know I've made it sound like we didn't enjoy each other's company, but that isn't true. Mother loved weekends away. At first, mainly on coach trips and then she encouraged me to learn how to drive as soon as I was old enough, so we had more freedom.

Most evenings, she would sit in the parlour watching the telly, mainly dramas and plays, though she enjoyed a good film from what she called her 'era'. The radio, her main form of entertainment, was on whenever she was busy in the kitchen. I would sit in the study, among the books, reading most evenings, a habit of mine left over from my school and university exams days. If there wasn't much on the telly Mother would retire to her bedroom early to write letters, saying, "Right, I'm off to bed now. Don't be late yourself; we can't afford the luxury of burning the midnight oil."

I never understood what she meant by the midnight oil, when we lived in the 1960s. I'm sure the Victorians who once inhabited our house probably burnt a lot of it. We could afford oil every day of the week if we needed the stuff. With what I earned I could light up the whole house and still have change to spend. I guess it was force of habit with Mother not wanting to waste a single penny after Father left.

In the past she'd let rooms out on the top floors to students from the local nursing college to make ends meet, but as I got older she'd stopped doing it for some reason.

Though Mother wasn't a churchgoer she had strict rules. Never allowing the students to have their boyfriends in their rooms, no smoking, or loud music, all rubbish to be brought down when leaving the house. The stairs had to be kept clear at all times and no canoodling on the front door step.

"I'm not running a brothel here," she would shout to anyone spending too long saying goodbye to their boyfriends. That word was the closest Mother came to swearing.

The only phone in the house was in the hall. Mother made it clear it was only to be used to call their family members. If any of the students needed to make a longer call, they had to use the telephone box on the corner. Mother would only take calls on their behalf if they came from a family member. We used to laugh about the fact that the girls all seemed to have a large number of brothers.

For a while I was the envy of all the boys at my school for having a group of stunning young women running around the place, filling it with laughter and excited chatter. The washing line was always full of brightly coloured clothes and skimpy underwear.

Oh, how I wish I could revisit those fun filled days,

17

those bright summer days so long ago. They seemed too magical to be real. I used to find jobs to do around the garden so I could watch the girls sunbathing; the ones that didn't go home for the weekend.

One hot summer, when I was about fourteen, dressed only in my shorts, I pretended to be trimming back a hedge, having got out a wheelbarrow and a pair of secateurs. As I snipped I glanced over my shoulder. Rosie, a tall, leggy, blonde, sat on a sun lounger watching me over the top of her sunglasses whilst rubbing lotion into her legs. I turned and she recapped the bottle she was holding.

"Your father must have been a good looking fellow, Harold?" Rosie said.

"My father," I stepped forward. "How do you know what my father looked like?"

She threw her head back, laughing, not unkindly, but still it made me blush.

"Oh, dear Harold, look at yourself in the mirror, and you'll see those long lashes, green eyes and thick hair. You'll be a heartbreaker for sure."

"Mother says only vain people spend time looking at themselves," I shot back. "Anyway, I don't know what he looked like."

She studied me pulling her glasses clear from her face. "Are you serious?" she asked. "Haven't you ever seen a photo of your father?"

I shook my head and moved closer to get a good view of her breasts.

She leant back lifting her legs up onto the lounger. "That's sad," she said, sweeping her hair off her shoulders so the sun could get to them too.

"Hey Rosie I hope you're browning nicely all over," a voice suddenly shouted from the attic window, "and not just cooking on one side."

"No Joni," she called back, her eyes never leaving my face.

She sat forward again her soft breasts moving. They reminded me of newly-hatched chicks in a nest, like the ones I'd found in the hedge at the bottom of the garden. Like them I had wanted to reach out and touch them to feel their soft, fluffy down, but I knew I mustn't because I couldn't bear them to suffer rejection by their mother in the same way as I had by my father.

"Hey, Smiler!"

I blinked lifting my eyes to her face. Suddenly realising Rosie was holding out the bottle of sun lotion to me. I took it but my hands were shaking.

"Could you do my back?" she said rolling onto her stomach and lifting her hair from her shoulders. "Don't get any in my hair, will you?"

She flinched when I squeezed the first dollop onto her.

"Oh, that was cold. Strange it should be so cold on such a hot day."

She chatted on, but I wasn't listening, my mind focusing on the cream as I worked it into her soft skin. It felt so warm to the touch. I closed my eyes wanting it to last forever.

While Mother lay dying I studied her leathery skin and recalled the warmth and softness of Rosie's under my fingertips. Mother's seemed far too tight to fit her frame any more, lying taut over her face giving it that death's head look. Her breathing seemed to answer the wind which shook the branches of the trees outside her bedroom window. Every breath became a battle as her life left her.

Once in a distant summer when Mother's skin had been soft and vibrant to the touch, had she smiled up at my father offering him not just a bottle of sun lotion but permission to touch her? Had he rubbed cream onto her back? Taking

19

his time with each gentle caress, enjoying every sensation coursing through his body, as I did on that day so long ago? Had she cooed to my father in the same way as Rosie did? Her voice soft and sweet?

As that teenager I wondered if sex was the same. The soft gentleness of skin against skin, the warmth of one person touching another and the sweetness of that lingering touch as you inched your way across the boundaries from decency to indecency. As I moved my hand across Rosie's back I'd tried to imagine what it would be like to touch her breasts, or the tops of her legs.

"Thank you, Harold, that's enough." Rosie stared at me through narrowing eyes. I froze and stared down at my hand. That's when I noticed the tightness in the front of my shorts. I looked up in time to see Mother storming across the garden. Her face a mask of suppressed fury made me drop the bottle. I rushed past her into the house just as her raised voice clashed with Rosie's.

Love and sex are two of the most powerful emotions on the earth. These feelings overwhelm us throughout our short lives. We squander them and by the time we're old enough to fully understand them, to enjoy them with our one true love, our bodies betray us, leaving just the ghosts of our passion.

Mother never explained any of this to me.

"You'll find out soon enough, Harold. And believe me you'll be just as disappointed as I was. Love and sex aren't all they're cracked up to be."

Once, in a moment of temper, I snapped at her wanting to know more. I was seventeen and in love with a girl who I worshipped from afar. I remember clearly her stunning eyes, silky hair and the way her lips always held a playful smile, unlike Mother's whose pursed lips suppressed in fury at the slightest mention of love and romance. I wanted so much to ask the girl out, but always lost my nerve.

One morning while at breakfast, I said, "I'm in love."

"Love!" Mother had snorted, as she placed a rack of toast before me. "You know nothing of love but what you read in your books. And, they call it romance."

"Have you ever been in love, Mother?"

"Don't get clever with me, lad," she had snapped. "I've been around too many years not to know what I'm talking about."

I stared at my plate. "Didn't you love Father?"

She sighed heavily and picked up the linen basket. As she went out the back door, she said, "I know I love you."

It was the only time she told me she loved me in words. It's funny but toast always makes me think of her love. At times it could be warm and comforting when you are too ill to eat anything else. Yet cold toast can be brittle and inedible, the last thing you want to eat on a frosty morning.

Mother made sure I got a good education, sending me to one of the posher schools in our area. How she could afford it, I never knew. She always attended the parents' evenings; smartly dressed her hair neat, fingernails clean. She would smile a lot and always spoke beautifully, sounding just as posh as everyone else there.

When meeting my teachers she would always announce, "I do apologise for Harold's father not being here but unfortunately he works abroad."

I would sit biting my lip whenever I heard her make that statement. I hoped the teachers would question her perhaps asking *Where was he? What did he do? How long was he expecting to be abroad for? And why I never spend my holidays with him?* But they never did. I knew better than to ask those sorts of questions for myself.

The boys in my class were like all boys. For whatever

21

reasons only known to them they had a habit of singling out anyone that was different. Of course my absent father, a mysterious figure, was a good enough reason for selecting me.

One day while we were all in the library studying in silence, Michael, the classroom bully unexpectedly asked, "What does your father do for a living, Harold?"

I inhaled sharply. All eyes turned in my direction. I continued to stare at my exercise book as the collective group held their breath.

"Bet he's in prison?" Roger, the fat boy stated, glad for once not to be in the line of fire.

"No, of course not." I focused on the words I'd just read. "He works abroad."

"Maybe he's a convict and was sent to Australia," Michael said, making the group snigger.

I met his defiant stare. "Well, if that's the case, then he's been dead a long time. If you'd listened in class you'd know they stopped sending convicts there in 1868."

"So you don't have a father then?" Roger asked.

"Of course, he does. We all do, but unlike us, Harold doesn't know who his father is," Michael said while pointing his pencil at me.

"He's a bloody bastard then." Roger was growing in confidence.

"You could be right, Fatso," Michael said, regaining his authority. Roger tried to conceal his blush by hiding behind his book.

"I'm not a bastard." I narrowed my eyes meeting Michael's stare.

"Prove it then." Michael's voice carried weight. "Let's see some family photographs. If you've a father we all want to know what he looks like. Don't we, lads?"

The class broke into catcalling.

"Is that all? You only had to ask."

Michael stared in disbelief his confidence waning.

"So do you want to see now?"

"Of course, dumb-arse. Go on, show us."

I pushed my chair back and stood. The room descended into silence.

"Well, just look at me." I held my arms up in a sweeping gesture. "I'm handsome like my father and unlike yours. If you're made in his image, Michael."

Michael's eyes dropped. He ran his tongue over his buckteeth. I knew I'd hit a nerve. I wasn't proud, just glad it shut him up. I gathered up my belongings heading back to my form room. By home time I hated Mother for not being honest about Father. I crashed through the back door, furious, knowing she would be in the kitchen. I dumped my bag on the floor and demanded to see a photo of my father.

She turned slowly colour draining from her face. Her legs shook so much they seemed unable to take her weight. I grabbed a chair and guided her to it, before fetching a glass of water.

"I'm so sorry." I knelt before her. "It's the boys at school. No, just that horrible kid, Michael, the one I've told you about before."

She reached out, brushing my fringe back as though I was a small child again.

"You know nothing," she said. "It won't end there. You think you're giving them what they want, but it won't be enough."

With that she patted my shoulder, stood and went back to peeling the vegetables for dinner. I had lost again.

School life was tough, but after that it became tougher still. Mother's lesson in life, I guessed. But all I'd learnt was that we were different from other families. My life was a never-ending lie. Mother told me nothing, while I deceived to the world. At least it kept her happy.

Then she died.

After all these years, I'm still shocked to find that no one mourns her passing, just the Vicar and me. Oh and God too, I suppose. Not that Mother was a great believer. As I sat, drinking tea in our tidy kitchen, I wished we'd moved to a smaller place with more of a community. Would Mother's life have been different? Maybe she would've made real friends. Maybe I wouldn't have been an only child if she had met someone else.

I sipped my drink while deciding what to do next. It dawned on me now was the time to find out about my father. I set my cup down and headed to her bedroom. Lurking within that secret domain was all the answers to my life-long questions. My heart pounded in my chest as I reached the bottom of the stairs. Lingering, I stared upwards, one foot hovering. Suddenly I wondered whether it was important to know after all.

"Maybe he's a man Mother needed to forget?" I heard myself saying, realising for the first time it wasn't all about me. Maybe I was a constant reminder of someone she wanted to forget? She'd been a good mother, kind and thoughtful. I never went without. Birthdays and Christmases were as special as they could be when there was just the two of us.

Slowly I began to climb, drawing in long deep breaths; a thought gnawed at my soul. Mother might've been thorough in other ways too destroying all paperwork and photos of the man she wanted to forget. Torn between the need to know the truth and whether my mother had kept anything pertaining to him I pushed all thoughts aside and continued to climb.

Halfway up the doorbell rang. I paused not expecting

anyone. So for a moment, I wondered if it's just my imagination.

Then it rang again. Confused I descended wondering idiotically if it was Mother putting an end to my quest.

On opening the door I was hurled back to my childhood. A woman stood in the semi-darkness of the porch, a younger version of Mother. The sound of her voice didn't match the image in my head. My mouth locked as questions crammed my mind.

"Oh God, Harold, we're so sorry just to turn up like this, but we missed you at the crematorium. We wanted a word with the vicar before—" Her voice was soft and gentle with a hint of an accent. "We're—" she looked over her shoulder. Out of the darkness a man appeared behind her.

I coughed clearing my throat, "You'd better come in, I'm not—" I stepped back, letting them pass.

"Running a brothel," they said together.

It was a joke but no one laughed. I stared in disbelief at the man an older version of myself.

"We're so sorry. Mum's last letter never reached us soon enough."

"Mum's?" I heard myself saying.

"Valerie the boy's in shock," the man said, opening the sitting room door. "Is it all right, if we all sit down in here?"

I nodded.

He smiled a familiar smile.

"I'll put the kettle on," Valerie said.

"No, love I'll do that. Take the lad in there. We've a lot of explaining to do."

"The kitchen is—" I pointed."

"It's all right. I know my way."

Puzzled I followed Valerie into the living room.

"Oh my – nothing has changed at all," she said.

"You've been here before?"

She turned. There was sadness in her eyes. "She kept her word, didn't she? You don't know?"

"Who are you? What's going on?" I was a child again with too many unanswered questions.

She crossed to the sideboard and studied Mother's collection of framed photographs. Most are of me alone, though there were a few taken on our trips of us together. I knew them all off by heart.

She selected one of me as an awkward teenager, brown-limbed, sitting with Rosie and Joni in the summer sunshine. As she set the picture carefully down again, she said, "You're a good looking lad."

"Please explain what's going on?" I asked.

The door banged open. The man returned carrying a tray. He set it down and dropped into Mother's chair. I looked away. It didn't seem right.

Valerie perched on the edge of the sofa while pouring the tea. After a moment she studied me and then with a nod, she asked, "Do you take sugar?"

"One please."

"It seems strange us not knowing," she passed me the cup.

"Why should you?" I stirred my tea.

She glanced towards the man her eyes filling with tears. "Dear God, where do we begin?"

He leant forward and took her hand. "Look, Harold, we… I… there's no better way of saying this, so I'll say it straight. We're your parents."

I exhaled. His words rattled around in my brain. "My parents?" Now this I hadn't expected. Not just a father but a new mother too. "No – that's not right. Mother would've said."

"I understand your confusion, but let us explain."

I stared at the woman who nodded.

"Valerie is your mother," the man continued, "the daughter of Jeannie Summerfield. Jeannie, who you knew as Mother, was in fact your grandmother."

"This isn't what we wanted, Harold. Not to tell you like this. Mum wrote to us so we knew what the doctor had said about not being able to treat her. Though she didn't know how long she had left and was desperate for us all to be together when we explained everything to you."

"We didn't want to tell you over the phone, lad," the man interposed.

"Why now?" I felt I was losing everything, my mother, my childhood were all lies. "Why wait until she's dead? Why not, when I was five, ten, or even eighteen?"

Colour drained from Valerie's face and I saw Mother before me.

"Oh Harold. When Mum's last letter arrived we'd been delayed in Northern Australia. We caught the next plane out hoping to see her before she passed away but once again fate intervened. The vicar who took the service is an old friend of David's father. He knew all about Jeannie's past and contacted us."

"Oh great so I'm the last to know?"

"That's unfair. He couldn't break his word to Jeannie by telling you about us,"

"Please?" Valerie pleaded.

I leant back. "I guess I've waited long enough."

Valerie let out a low sigh, and said, "David and I have known each other since childhood…"

"Oh, how very nice for you."

"Please listen to what your mother has to say—"

"My mother is dead. I've just come back from her funeral."

"We were there too. We know you're hurting but you

need to understand. She wasn't your mother but your grandmother," David said.

I could see he was trying to hold it together but I was angry about losing my mother, and now my very identity too. "I'm sorry, am I supposed to just – what? Eradicate the last twenty-four years of my life on your word? Explain, if you can?"

David offered Valerie a hanky. After she wiped her eyes she took a deep breath. "At fourteen I fell in love and became pregnant. Like all mothers Mum wanted the best for me. *Education is the key that set women free. It allows them to make choices for themselves.* Something she'd hammered into me from an early age. So when I threw away the opportunity she'd worked so hard for, to be with David, well – it broke her heart."

"You're saying she threw you out but kept me?" I stared at the pictures on the sideboard. The familiar face of my mother stared back at me.

"No she forgave me. For a time we lived here happily. After you were born David and I wanted a place of our own. At seventeen his wages couldn't support us so when an opportunity came to serve an apprenticeship with a large company in Scotland – he took it."

"I wanted to take you both with me," David said, "but Jeannie wanted Valerie to finish her education first. So I left on my own. Valerie, like your grandmother, is bloody-minded." He grinned at her. She smiled back but it didn't quite reach her eyes.

"I just couldn't live without him," she said, "so I ran away."

"And left me behind?"

"We understand that you feel we deserted you," David said. "But you need to understand we had no choice. With no money and just a one-way train ticket to Scotland we

28

had no idea where we would be sleeping. It seemed the best thing for you to stay with Jeannie, until we knew where we would be living."

"David worked long hours and I worked when I could," Valerie said.

"Your mum was under age so the only jobs she could do were cash in hand, no questions asked. On pay days we could just about afford to pay the rent on our small room and feed ourselves."

"At first Mum thought I would return once things became difficult," Valerie said.

"So she knew where you were?" I asked.

"Yes Harold. The agreement was Mum would look after you until we got ourselves settled."

"That's when my company dropped a bombshell. They decided to relocate to Australia. I had no choice but to go," David continued. "At eighteen Valerie made the choice to come with me. We came to see you before we left. You were settled and already calling Jeannie 'Mummy'. Difficult times for us all but a hopeful one too."

"So Mother never lied. My father did work abroad."

Valerie nodded. "It seemed so unfair to lose Mum now we can be together as a family. I thought losing everything in a bush fire was bad enough, but this—" She began weeping again.

"What about me?" I asked.

"Sorry?"

"You left me with someone who was incapable of loving."

"What?" Valerie rose from the sofa. "How can you say that of your grandmother?"

"Shh Valerie," David turned to me. "You've no idea what went before. We understand you're hurting, feeling betrayed, but it is nothing compared to what happened to your grandmother. As a young girl she escaped from an abusive home only to find herself working in a brothel."

"A brothel? As a whore!"

"Never ever call her that again. Do you hear me?" David shouted.

I nodded, feeling my cheeks redden.

"She had no choice after finding herself pregnant at fifteen. She feared her baby would be taken into care. She came to my father's church asking for help. Jeannie never told my parents what she did for a living only that she *burnt the midnight oil* and needed a safe place to leave her daughter while working. My mother, Pat, agreed to help and refused to take any payments Jeannie offered. Mother encouraged her to educate herself and lent her books in exchange for looking after Valerie. In time she'd saved enough to buy this house, hoping by letting rooms she could pay for her daughter's education at a good school."

"Instead she paid for me," I said realising why education was so important to my... grandmother... it seemed unnatural to say even in my mind.

"Yes." David smiled, reflecting my own smile back at me.

"Once I was told that my father must've been a good looking man because I took after him," I said laughing. "I guess that was true, Dad."

He stood wrapping his strong arms around me.

"We're so sorry, son. Everything seemed stacked against us. I can't begin to tell you how much I've wanted to hear you call me Dad."

Then my mother, my real mother, embraced us both. "It's time we became a family," she whispered. "You'll return with us, won't you?"

"What about my home here?"

"Your grandmother asked me to give you this," Valerie said tears rolling down her cheeks.

I recognised the all too familiar blue airmail paper. Not in a million years would I have guessed she was writing to my parents. With trembling hands I tore open the envelope and began to read.

Dearest Harold,

My darling grandson finally all your many questions will be answered by those who should explain all. I've longed for the right time to come when we would all be together, but unfortunately fate was against us. Now it is your time to decide. You can stay or sell the house, but it must be your choice whether you begin a fresh life in a new country with your parents or not.

Your ever-loving grandmother,
Jeannie.

As the plane takes off I stare down on England knowing I shall never return. Before me is a lifetime of discoveries as I get to know my parents. But what I really want to know and understand for myself is how powerful love can be.

The Newcomers

As we leave behind all that was once familiar to us the thunder rumbles across the darkening sky. High above us lightning flashes slicing through the black clouds, arcing against a tall tree and splitting it in two just as we pass by. At last, we can smell rain in the air after the heat of another long day.

For the last few cycles of the sun the remnants of what was once my pride has been on the move. Our only respite being when hunger and thirst drives us to search for food and any water we are lucky enough to find in this barren, unfamiliar land.

I look back over my shoulder and see my mother, Soraya, with her head down as she pants in the endless heat. She makes slow, but steady progress, with my two sisters, Halala and Mari, flanking her on either side.

I shiver with fear at the unfamiliar landscape stretching out before us. I pause long enough to allow my family to catch up and to feel the darkness closing in. My body shakes violently as I recall those who are no longer with us.

Suddenly the long awaited rain begins to fall. Lightly at first it barely wets the dry ground and is no more than a promise. I carry on walking wanting to find somewhere safe for us before night falls. Another crack of thunder echoes overhead and the heavens open. The rain heavy now is running in rivulets down my body and frees my matted fur from the blood of my clan, cleansing me of all that had gone before.

I turn my head to lick my rain-soaked shoulder and glance back checking on the progress made by the others. I'm shocked to find Mother sitting alone, cleaning the wound to her shoulder, while my sisters are nowhere to be seen.

Wearily I retrace my steps coming alongside of her, I ask, "What is wrong? Where are my sisters?"

"Worry not child of mine," she says. "I needed to rest for just a moment."

Within her tired eyes I see the devastating effect the last few cycles of the sun have caused. Mother shakes her head and pulls at her fur as she licks the weeping wound.

Nervous for our safety I glance at the shadows moving within the fading light of the unfamiliar place. Sensing my concerns Mother stops her licking. "Child of mine we need to rest. Your sisters have gone looking for food." She's no longer the patient one. "We're all tired."

"But Mother we must keep moving, if we are to find sanctuary." As my impatience grows I paw at the ground and growl. "We need to stay together at all times."

My trepidation is now bubbling to the surface and I sniff the air as I begin to pace, recalling the bloody massacre we suffered a few cycles of the sun ago. Mother senses my fears and nuzzles against me trying to reassure me that my sisters will return. My concerns subside. I respond to her affection by pushing my head into her neck. She turns her proud head up to the rain and lets out a deep painful roar of anguish. I feel my heart breaking as I join her in her pain knowing that she hides her tears among the raindrops that splatter her scarred face.

No more than twenty-eight cycles of the sun ago I had woken to feel the coolness of an early morning. In the far distance a sliver of the sun was just visible through the darkness on the horizon. I arched my back and shook out my legs one by one. As my pride slept on I stepped gingerly over the smallest of my cubs. He squeaked softly in his sleep but did not stir as I wandered down to the waterhole. After taking my fill of the muddy water I glanced around at the shadowy figures. Their low grumbling told me they were wildebeest and the quiet ones were their companions, the zebras. I ran my tongue over my teeth feeling the fine grit between them and longing for the rains to fall so I could taste fresh water again.

I moved away from the waterhole and sensed the uneasiness running through the wildebeests and their companions. Not just because of my presence but more because of their impatience to be on their pilgrimage as they went in search for the lush, green grasses in our vast continent.

For the last few cycles of the sun I had watched for signs of their exodus as our waterhole began to shrink. All manner of beasts gathered at its edge in the growing heat of the day. The diversity of my landscape astounded me. I looked across the endless plains where my ancestors have roamed for hundreds of years before the Newcomers came.

As I climbed up onto the rocky outcrop my three playful cubs greeted me with pitiful shrieks nudging me to feed them. I lay on my side and they eagerly scrambled up onto my belly latching on with their sharp tiny teeth. I took comfort from knowing that I had plenty of milk to feed my growing family and delighted in their squeaks as they fed.

I took my time enjoying the peacefulness of that morning. My tail flicked constantly brushing away buzzing flies. As the sun warmed the air, my pride stirred in the growing heat ready to face the hectic time ahead before the sun sets once more.

My three sisters, Mari the elder, Halala and Ebony, were busy feeding their cubs, while my uncles, brothers of Nama, my father and our leader, set off to mark the borders of our territory with the pride's odour, spraying it on bushes, trees and across the ground so others knew it belonged to us. Across the sweeping savannah the restless herds of gazelles, buffalo, and giraffes fed on the last remaining green shoots while on the far horizon I watched as a herd of elephants, with their young following behind, came into view. They moved in time to the same rhythmical beat that echoed through all who inhabited this ancient land.

Our hearts beat in time to the rhythm of the landscape carried on the light summer breezes which shook the dried grass seed heads. The same rhythm had been heard a millennium or more ago by the forebears of all those who shared the vast wilderness with us. From chatting flocks of migrating birds to the sounds of the grunting wildebeest and the trumpeting elephants as they called their excited youngsters back into line.

Not far behind the elephants I watched the rhinos lead their youngsters to the same shrinking waterhole to drink. Suddenly the ground began to quake a sound rumbled across the savannah and echoing around the outcrop waking my pride. We all stood to watch as the thunderous hooves of wildebeest and zebras told us all of their leaving.

"Come Riyal, quickly. The herds are on the move!"

Mari's call shook me out of my reverie. I gently licked each one of my cubs in turn enjoying the smell of their milky softness before I nudged them away. I joined my sisters knowing our cubs would be well cared for by our mother and their aunt while we were out hunting.

We moved through the trees and bushes to the far side of the waterhole on the outer edges of the drying marshland. Mari took the lead her fine lean back shone in the dappled light while I followed at the rear. Heading for our familiar hunting ground, we passed a few nervous wildebeests and zebras as they churned up dust and the dried grass desperately looking for something to eat.

Instinctively, without calling, gesturing or signalling to each other we knew our plan of attack. Ebony, with her

35

head down, moved away to the right disappearing among the trees as I broke off to slip around behind my sister, Halala. Mari moved to the far side of the marshland to watch the zebras as they nervously came looking for water.

Finally, after hours of waiting in the heat, a small herd of zebras broke free. In desperation their thirst had forced them to overcome their fears about approaching the waterhole. Shortly what we had hoped and waited for happened. One of them became too engrossed in chewing the moist greener grass that edged the water.

I could see Halala's muscles taut against her fur as her eyes locked on to the prey. Once it was far enough away from the safety of the herd she matched her movement to that of the zebra only stopping when it looked up. Her muscles rippled with concentration making her twitch snake-like amongst the grasses. Ebony and I joined her as she melted into the background. Mari moved forwards on her belly her nose glistening in the sun as she steadied her breathing.

As soon as the zebra relaxed enough to continue feeding, we all shifted our positions, moving forward as one closing the gap between our prey and us. We inched our way forward on our bellies turning our paws over to deaden the sound of our movements in the dry grass. Fearing our pride may not eat today we all froze. The young zebra sensing movement looked up again.

Excitement overtook our hungry bellies as Mari crashed out from the undergrowth propelled forward at high speed by her powerful hind legs. For a moment our prey froze as Halala and I came into view cutting it off from the rest of its herd. On finding its escape route blocked the zebra hesitated, crying for help. It then charged at us as Ebony appeared from nowhere.

Sensing its change in direction Halala sprung backward twisting her body in mid-air and gave chase. In the growing heat not wanting to waste any more energy I charged after it. My chest tightened as my heart pounded knowing that the zebra could easily outrun us. Halala tried to grab its back legs but it kicked out. Suddenly, Ebony sunk her hooked claws in, dragging it down as Halala went for its neck, biting through its throat, and cutting off its air supply.

It was all over. Death came quickly. The zebra died with honour. We tore into it filling our empty bellies and then carried the rest back to our pride. On seeing us returning with a kill our father roared his delight. The resonance of his voice created a wall of sound that crossed our lands letting others know of his power and command as he took control of our kill. Moments later I heard my uncles answering his calls closely followed by the roars from other prides' protectors that surrounded our borders. After Nama took his fill he joined the rest of us as we lazed in the shade of the outcrop worn out by our hunt and the heat. As my eyes grew heavy I gathered my cubs to me.

In the distance a growing dust cloud rose up into the clear blue sky telling me the thundering feet of the wildebeests had begun to leave our territory. As I lay sleeping I felt something pushing at my shoulder. Fearing for my cubs I let out a low roar and gathered them to me.

"Hush child of mine."

"Mother what is it?"

"Someone comes. Wake your sisters."

I stood sniffing the air. In the distance I could see the intruders moving swiftly towards us. Hastily I rounded the boulders that separated me from my sleeping sisters and their cubs and began to nudge them awake. My mother and aunts' roars filled the air with warning sounds.

As my sisters and I gathered our cubs and carried them one at a time to the safety of the long dried grasses to hide them our father bellowed. His roars ricocheted around us.

Mari nuzzled me. "What is going on? Who are they?" I shook my head looking back over my shoulder. "Mother seems fearful. Something is not right."

"We'll look after your little ones, Riyal, while you go and find out," Halala said, carrying my smallest son in her mouth, and placing him next to hers. With playful swipes of their paws they tumbled with each other. We adults worried for them knowing that if the intruders were not family they would die.

I clambered back up to the outcrop pausing for a moment to watch my sisters move our children further away. From the top ridge in the fading light I saw Nama standing with his back raised and his mane billowing out as he tossed his powerful head from side to side while his tail flicked.

Just behind him my mother and two aunts stood with their hackles raised; something was unquestionably wrong. In the distance the two approaching figures suddenly became recognisable. I was shocked when I realised they were my uncles.

Nama raised his hackles, arched his back and stamping his massive paws. He roared. The sound echoed around us chilling me to the core. With an enormous leap he crashed onto the ground before them.

"Wait!" Mother shook her own head roaring at my aunts as they were about to rush forward, snarling and gnashing their teeth. My aunts lowered their heads and pawed impatiently at the ground while voicing their anger with rumbling growls. Nama towered over my uncles stopping them in their tracks.

"Where have you been, fools?" he roared spraying spittle over them as they cowered before him. "You stink of the Newcomers. I could smell you miles away!" He swung his huge right paw catching Uncle Remus across his left eye.

With blood trickling down his cheek uncle lowered his head before lying down.

"I told you both before to stay well away from them!" Nama bellowed.

Meekly Uncle Atticus rolled on to his back baring his belly to show his attrition as he tried to appease our protector.

Nama stepped forward. "What's your excuse this time, Atticus?"

"My Lord," Atticus sat up, but kept his head lowered in submission as he eyed Nama's paws. "The wildebeest have started to leave us and our children will starve. The Newcomers have plenty enough to share with us-" he paused as Nama stepped forward.

"Go on for I feel you have more to say—"

"I think it's only fair that they share with us as we've shared with them. Do they not hunt on our lands, take the fish from our lakes and birds from our sky?" He gave a nervous growl.

After Remus finished wiping the wound to his cheek he added, "They've moved into our territory taking what belongs to us away. We're not cowards. We should make a stand and drive them back as we do with the nomads who threaten our pride."

Nama threw his head back his mane seeming to double in size. "You stupid fools!" he bellowed. "The nomads understand the rules of our society. The Newcomers do not! They see wide empty spaces." He gestured with a sweep of his paw. "But they do not see us. They see land in which to colonise but they do not smell our borders. What are we to them? We have no real value."

He glared down at his quaking brother. "To them we are dangerous creatures that will devastate their lives and destroy their cattle. And now you two have proven them right."

"The Newcomers are weak creatures that we can easily overcome," Remus said, with a shake of his head.

Mother stepped forward, "Dear Remus Nama is right. You are the fool. Weak indeed they maybe but you've made us a target now. The hunters have fire-sticks to protect them. They see us as nothing more than a trophy. For generations my bloodlines have hunted these lands. The Newcomers have left us alone as we were of no threat to them but now – who knows what will happen?" Now that the sun had sunk below the far horizon I saw flashes of lights moving in our direction as Nama and my uncles roared at each other with dissatisfaction. "Father. Mother. Something is coming our way! Look they are moving faster than elephants!" I bellowed, jumping down from the outcrop and pushing my way between them.

Father snarled at me. His hot breath in my face made me wince as he swept me aside with his huge paw as he continued to roar at Remus.

The first shot seemed to light up the darkness. It echoed around the rocks and boulders of our dusty lair. For a moment nothing happened. Nama, drawing himself up, began to roar and bellow again as he thundered off into the night towards the ever-growing bright lights. I stood stunned unsure what I should do next as my uncles crashed after him all their differences forgotten as they reacted to his cries to protect the pride.

"Go back, child of mine," Mother snarled at me. "Find your sisters quickly. Take as many cubs as you can. The Newcomers will kill us all!"

I heard Father and the uncles' roars and snarls echoing around us. Dazed by the melee I was rooted with fear with Mother's words ringing in my ears – *the Newcomers, the Newcomers; the two-legged ones who will kill all of us.*

Nama roared at us to leave our territory when a loud

bang rung out and his roaring ceased. Mother turned to me just as we heard several more loud bangs. The cries of my uncles died away too.

"Go quickly my child. Go!" She pushed me into action.

"But Mother what of you?"

"Quickly go before they come this way!"

I jumped onto the outcrop moving rapidly as I hunted for my sisters. The sounds of the Newcomers' vehicles echoed around us. I heard Mother roaring at them and realised she was trying to lead them away. I moved on my belly making cub-like mewls in the darkness. I cried out to my sisters when I heard Mari.

"Riyal over here."

As I came to her she licked my cheek and then brushed against the full length of my body before rubbing her face against mine. "What's happening?" she whispered.

"The Newcomers are here to kill us. Our uncles killed their cattle. I think Father and the uncles are dead. We must leave!"

"What of our mother?"

"I don't know -" I sobbed. "She said we must leave taking as many of our -" I paused, sniffing the air. An unfamiliar smell filled my nostrils which wasn't the smell of jackals or hyenas.

On the night breeze, mixed in with the barking of dogs, Halala roared. Terror filled the air as the sound of plaintive cries from our unprotected cubs came from all directions. Mari followed the sounds.

I came from the other direction. Together we hunted in the long dried grasses for our cubs. My heart broke when I found the first one of Halala's cubs the one who moments before had played with my smallest. His broken body smelt of blood and dogs. I pressed my nose to the ground and followed the trail of broken bodies roaring with anguish at the moon when the next one was one of my own. No more could I smell the sweet milky softness of my cubs over that of the spilt blood.

My uncles were right. We had gained nothing from the Newcomers as their numbers increased. They spread, disease-like, across the land and with them comes death and destruction. While our freedom shrinks.

The sounds of the barking dogs and the Newcomers leached away into the darkness. I searched among the trampled grasses for signs of my sisters and any surviving cubs but fearing I'm the only survivor.

My heart lifted when I detected the smell of Ebony. I rushed forward only to discover, in a clearing, her savaged body pressed up against a wall of rock. Surrounding her were the torn bodies of her cubs.

I licked all that remained of her once kind face. The dogs had torn her lips away exposing her teeth. Her dead eyes stared in an unanswered plea of forgiveness at the loss of our cubs. I followed the scent of the dogs vocalising the anger within me. Back at the outcrop I climbed up and took my father's place to roar my grief at the moon until my strength failed me. Exhausted I collapsed onto the rock and slept.

I woke to nudging, and rolled onto my back expecting my hungry cubs needed feeding. When the sweet pain of the tiny teeth never happened I opened my eyes and saw the bloodied face of my mother.

"Oh sweet child of mine," she sobbed. "I thought you were dead too."

"Mother they are all gone. Ebony is dead too."

She licked the tears from my eyes as I became aware of the darkening morning sky. A swirling black mass echoed with the sound of cawing as vultures descended to squabble over the carnage that had once been our pride, our family.

As Mother and I watched the clattering of falling rocks made us both turn with hackles raised ready to fight. Instead we let out a deep sob as the two battle-scarred lionesses, Mari and Halala, stood before us.

Reluctantly we surrendered our territory to the Newcomers and moved deeper into the wilderness. All we could hope for now was to find another pride willing to accept female outsiders. My greatest fear was my mother's age was against her.

After twenty-eight cycles of the sun we'd passed through other territories unheeded until the storm broke. Mother refused to take another step. When, at last, the sun broke on the horizon, we found ourselves on a grassy open plain surrounded by mountains and swamplands. We delighted in drinking from a pool of clear water where we could see fish swimming. We hunted for food in the scattered woodland where the only animals we could smell were prey. I began to relax and enjoyed watching Mother regain her health. One bright morning I was shaken from my sleep by my sister Mari. "Come see, Riyal. Come see. We have visitors!"

As I followed her down the slope to the valley floor I became aware of Mother's playful roars. For a moment I thought Nama had returned. As I broke through the undergrowth the sight that confronted me was Mother tussling with a wiry, old male who towered over her. With playful roars he dodged the teasing swipes of her paws.

With squeals of delight Mari rushed forward to join them. I hung back watching Halala play-fighting with three other younger handsome males. I dropped to my belly and began to lick at my paws pretending disinterest in their games though I still glanced over occasionally in case things turned nasty.

As my eyes began to close a deep throaty roar from the

leaner of the younger males made me leap up in horror. I held my breath fearing the worst. Instead I saw the sheen of his glossy coat shining in the light. I wanted to join them and be part of what we had been before – a pride.

I rolled onto my back, and stretched. Through narrowing eyes I observed my sisters begin the ritual licking and grooming as they slowly accepted their new mates. I rolled over, closed my eyes, relaxing in the warm sunshine. I inhaled the fresh smell of the grass, knowing we were at last at our journey's end.

Suddenly a dark shadow passed over me. On opening my eyes I found the leaner of the younger males sniffing me.

"Hello, I'm Cango," he growled softly. "Aren't you joining us – err."

"Riyal. My name's Riyal." I lowered my head.

He began to lick my face and I found myself returning them. He grew braver and nipped at my ears and neck. He growled, "Come and join us."

It's been fourteen cycles of the sun since we formed our new pride. Some of our sorrow has retreated now that we live in the peaceful valley. Cango licks at my ears as my belly grows fatter. This time I hope to see my cubs fully grown so that I can teach them to recognise the signs and smells of the Newcomers and their dogs.

In turn they will pass on the instinct to their children so they will understand the dangers too. I know it will only be a matter of time when the disease we know as 'The Newcomers' spreads throughout all our lands and there will be nowhere left for us to go.

The Kite

In the clear night sky the moon hung high above. Like a silent watcher it cast long shadows over no-man's land. Harry stood, saturated by the heavy dew, peering over the trench walls, watching, knowing at last he could do his bit for King and Country.

For so long as he could remember he had hated the faceless enemies. Night after night with his rifle held high he watched. All around him the sounds of shells and gunshots thundered in the darkness punctuated only by the screams of dying men. For him there was only despair reflecting in the endless dips and hollows that pitted the once beautiful landscape caused by the shells as they tried to win back the land lost to them on other such nights. Sometimes he was sure he could hear laughter coming from the Germans' side above the sound of the big guns.

"Are they laughing at us, George?" Through clenched teeth Harry ground the words out to his comrade-in-arms before lifting his rifle higher and steadying his aim. "Good men are dying because of the likes of them? I see no fun in that!"

Anger tore through Harry's heart but his conscience would be clear. He would never allow another man to suffer, unlike the enemy. No, not until he stood before them, would he fire a single shot.

"I know," George said stifling a yawn. "But don't let them get to you." He patted Harry's shoulder as he squeezed past him. "I'm off to get some kip if the buggers let me."

At first light through the misty haze that hung over the few feet of no-man's-land Harry caught sight of ghostly shadows moving amidst the vapour. With aching muscles in his back, the tops of his arms and legs, he tightened his grip on his gun and steadied his aim. His chest and head knotted as his face grew hot, inflamed by the enemy's disregard of the raging turmoil around them. He watched as they lazily drew on their cigarettes, sending up clouds of smoke, while their muffled voices carried across the land tormenting him.

One night on watch Harry became aware that the man was pointing his gun at him. Wasn't it the same man who had been there on previous nights? Harry wasn't sure how he knew – he just did.

Was it the way the enemy stood, so still and unwavering in his aim? Maybe it was the way he held his rifle with just as much determination as he did? For that he respected him. Harry shivered, suddenly aware that some sort of familiarity had passed between them.

The days passed into weeks and the summer became autumn. The dried soil soon became a sea of mud as the rain mixed with the blood of men and horses. Bullets and bombs rained down on them along with the last of the falling leaves from the bullet-ridden trees that edged the trenches. The trees stood like wounded guardian angels with their limbs torn away as they tried and failed to protect the lost souls in their care. The stench of death mingled in the air along with the decaying leaves.

Harry stared at the trees and shivered touched by their sadness. They reminded him of the large ancient oak trees that edged meadows of an England lost to him now. Warmed by thoughts of home washing over him he tried to forget the damp that ate its way through the soles of his boots and crawled up his legs. He shivered again. This time touched by the coldness of the racing wind that whistled along the trenches in its bid to escape the surrounding madness.

"Here's something to break the monotony, Harry."

Startled out of his thoughts he turned to find George holding out a letter. "Thanks, George." He lowered his gun.

"God only knows what will kill us first – the boredom, stench, rats, or mud. Sometimes I doubt the enemy will get a look in. What do you think, Harry?" George called back over his shoulder as he squelched his way to the next man.

Harry wiped his hands on his jacket sleeves and using a penknife slit open the letter. Guilt flooded him with every word he read.

Dearest son,

I hope this letter finds you well. I'm sorry it's short but I've been busy helping in the fields. Dad has more than enough work to keep ten men going. It's been a good harvest this year with a high yield. Though Tom is getting to be a big lad he's not yet strong or tall enough to swing a scythe.

I'm hoping that I'll find the time to write you a good long letter soon.

Must go now my dearest Harry.

Watch out for a parcel. We sent one but maybe you have already received it? Please don't say you don't have time to write. Even if it's only a postcard I will be satisfied.

Dad and Tom send their love.

Keep safe and make haste to come home.

Mother

X

Harry folded the letter carefully and slipped it into a waxed paper envelope with the others. He tucked it into his breast pocket, hoping to keep them safe and dry, before picking up his gun again. As he focused on the enemy's line he reasoned his father needed him far more than his King did. Surely the country needed men to plough the fields and harvest the crops to feed them all during this time?

That last Sunday before being called up seemed a lifetime ago. The family had gone to church before they waved him off. They watched as he, with many other young men from their village, joined the other soldiers going to the local railway station. Harry could still feel the intensity of his mother's embrace as she kissed him goodbye. Tom, just a kid, at nine, was too young to fight for King and Country and of some help to his parents. Harry had been relieved that his mother would not lose both her sons to the war as she proudly stood waving him goodbye.

The hardest thing Harry had found was trying to snatch sleep at any time during the day or night. When given notice to leave his post he'd hurried dog-tired back to his bunk.

For shelter the bunk was carved into the trench wall but it hadn't the power to block out the noise to allow his body to slip peacefully into the arms of Morpheus. The world seemed to scream at him to stay and fight. When his exhausted body and mind finally gave in he dreamt of home.

The warmth of a sweetly perfumed summer breeze caressed his bare back as he bent; hoe in hand, to help his father. Tom, all thin arms and legs, ran like the wind he chased. He ran across the field at the back of the house with a homemade kite in tow. In the yard their mother stood, tall and slender, her black hair pinned up under a straw bonnet. At her hip she held a basket from which she tossed grain to the clucking chickens that gathered at her feet. Catching sight of the kite riding on the warm air currents above her head she shielded her eyes in time to see it dancing on the summer breeze.

Father straightened too and leant on his hoe to rest awhile. A deep chuckle broke the silence between them. "I see the lad has made another one. My, my, that boy has determination, I'll give him that." He patted Harry on his back and for a brief moment he felt his father's strength. "You, my lad, are strong both in mind and in character. I'm so proud of you both."

With that, his father carried on with his toil, as though nothing had happened. As the power of his father's love and pride flooded through him Harry felt himself smiling also knowing his father was not one for fancy words.

A terrifying scream tore Harry from his father's side as the dream faded. Startled awake he almost fell from his bunk. His breath caught in his throat as he lay stunned by the agonising noise. On trying to open his eyes his heart began to race, for something wet and sticky covered them causing sudden blindness.

At first, he thought, he was the one screaming as he wiped at his eyes. Now that he could see again he checked his hands and to his horror saw the blood. If it wasn't his where had it come from?

A scream rang out again, piercing, pitiful and nearby.

Harry peered over the side of his bunk. A boy lay in the mud.

"Tom?" he heard himself saying.

The boy's head turned slowly. Then with pleading baby-blue eyes and a lost expression he met Harry's gaze.

Harry stood trying to catch his breath.

The boy-child, no more than seventeen, lay where he had fallen. He sat against the wooden barge board in a mixture of mud and dirt from where the shell had blasted the trench wall. Between what was left of the boy's legs lay his severed arm in a pool of blood on the duckboards.

Harry sensed a sort of tranquillity, transfixed by the fallen boy, even though all around the big guns continued to rain chaos and hell fire down on them. There was no sign of pain or tears in the boy's eyes as Harry knelt beside him.

"Help me, Mister. I can't move my legs."

"I'm sorry, lad. There's nothing I can do but pray for you."

The boy closed his eyes.

Relief washed over Harry as the boy slipped away to somewhere far more peaceful. Then a low groan emanated from the boy as his eyes opened again. A sickening bile rose in Harry as he realised what he had to do. The boy suddenly spoke his thoughts aloud.

"Please kill me, Mister. I beg you. I can't stand the pain or noise anymore."

Harry offered up a silent prayer as the boy begun to cough up thick red blood which oozed from between pale lips. Without a second thought Harry lifted his revolver to the boy's head.

A gentle smile flickered across the boy's thin bloodless lips. "Oh thank you, Mister. I can go home now."

The sound of Harry's revolver echoed around the trench and seemed to block out the roar of the big guns. Harry lowered his gun as a tear rolled down his cheek.

"Poor sod, isn't much else we could've done for the little bugger." A voice said from behind him. Harry wiped his cheeks and flopped back on his bunk.

"Don't you worry; it's what the lad wanted. None of us should be that lucky. Come on George give us a hand. We'll see if we can find a hole somewhere for him. You've done enough, Harry. You're a braver man than I'll ever be."

Harry stared at the gun in his hand and tossed it away aware that he hadn't killed one of the faceless enemies but a boy. He pushed his revolver back in its holster, picked up his rifle and took his place back at his post. As he looked across no-man's-land he saw his enemy at his post his gun focused on him. No longer did Harry watch with a keen eye or hold his gun with a steady aim. He hadn't the stomach for it.

Laughter echoed along the trenches. Perplexed Harry looked around to see where it came from and curled his lips in disgust when he realised it came from his own trench.

"Had everyone forgotten so quickly? Are we so numbed by death that we no longer care about one of our own?"

He lifted his gun, and stared across to no-man's-land.

Confusion filled the blood-scented air as Harry became aware that his enemy was no longer staring at him, but up at the clear blue sky. He stood with his hand shielding his eyes from the autumn sun. Harry lowered his rifle and followed his gaze until he saw what had caught his attention.

There fluttering over no-man's-land, high in the sky, hanging on a light breeze was a white kite. Its brightly coloured tails seemed to dance in numerous twists and turns as the wind dipped and flowed.

Slowly along the trenches on both sides the men on the front line began to shield their eyes and look skywards before nudging their comrades to look. Harry followed the string to earth and found no one holding the kite. He checked the front line again reasoning aloud.

"Surely someone is holding it?"

Harry glanced towards his enemy. He gestured back to Harry with a shrug of his shoulders to show he too was puzzled. Harry found himself smiling and returned the gesture.

In that moment he wondered what else they shared. After all, they were both men with parents and maybe siblings too? Did he watch the kite in the same way as him? Had he spent time with his father, in a garden, in some other time and place?

Harry laid his gun down and climbed over the top of the trench. He walked towards the enemy line with his arms outstretched.

"Come back you stupid bastard! You'll get yourself killed!"

He heard his men calling, but he kept on walking. He passed the broken bodies of men from both sides, they littered the battlefield, as if the mud had tried and failed to swallow them up. They stared vacant-eyed at the hovering white kite with its crucifix-stylized cross made out of thin canes.

Suddenly the guns fell silent. Harry in the heart of no-man's-land stared up at the dancing kite. Out of the opposing trench came the familiar figure of the enemy. He walked towards him with his arms outstretched. In the middle of all the madness the two men embraced like old friends.

No words were spoken. There wasn't any language left to express the sorrow or anguish felt by them both. Harry's adversary took his hands in his pulling him onto his knees. Harry sensed what the unknown soldier wanted and placed his hands together and closed his eyes. He lifted his head towards heaven and offered up a prayer for all the lost souls. The man pulled Harry to his feet, then after embracing him tightly for a few moments, he held him at arm's length. Harry, bathed in an ethereal golden light, stared deep into the soldier's eyes. For the briefest of moments he saw the dancing kite with its fluttering multi-coloured tails reflected within them.

After the man embraced him again, he turned and walked away leaving Harry with a deep sense of peace. Just as Harry clambered back into his trench he glanced over his shoulder, and noticed that both the soldier and the kite were gone. He was stunned for a moment wondering if it had all been a dream. Then he became aware that the big guns with their dragon-like mouths roared fire into the sky as the sounds of war filled the air with death once more.

"Wake up, Daddy!" An excited child called as he rushed into the study from the garden.

"My darling, are you okay?" Harry's wife asked as she wrapped her arms around his neck.

"Daddy mustn't be late for church."

Harry opened his eyes slowly. His son stood before him with his hands resting on his father's knees as he smiled up at his father.

"Daddy, I knew you weren't asleep. You must be ready to go to work soon."

Harry laughed and sat up in his armchair before straightening his clerical collar.

"I'm fine my dear. I just felt a little tired." Harry stood and picked up his sermon. "I'm ready to go now, Thomas." Harry embraced his wife before lifting his son to kiss his cheek.

The memories of the war to end all wars would never leave him. He knew it had marked him in so many ways. As it had done many others, but he'd been one of the lucky few who had survived. He looked down into the eyes of his son and hoped he would never have to take another man's life for either the right or wrong reasons.

"After church, Daddy, can we fly my kite again?"

"Of course we can, Thomas." Harry ruffled Thomas' hair. "It looks to be the perfect day for it. Peaceful and just the right amount of summer breeze to make it dance."

On the Streets of Kabul

Between the dust, sand, heat and the flies the sweat trickled down my face and ran down the back of my neck as fear pounded in my heart overtaking everything. Still I'm the lucky one. Only one day left of this war for me; only one more day of its madness. Come tomorrow I'll be free from it forever.

On the streets of Kabul everyone is your enemy. You trust no one. I can't wait to walk casually down Civvy Street without wearing a gun. To never again have to glance over my shoulder every second and to know that an open smiling face is an offer of friendship and not hidden hostility.

For now I must stay focused and get the job in hand done. They call it the 'War on Terror' but they don't know the half of it. We sit with our backs against a crumbling bullet-riddled wall as incoming fire whistles all around.

We count the minutes, while looking skywards, longing for the familiar sound of the copters' blades whooshing overhead and hoping it'll free us from the shit-hole we're trapped in. I stare at the ground in front of me sinking deeper inside my flak jacket as the blistering heat drains my energy. Normality stares back at me as the ants scurry around minding their own business. What do they know or care about the struggles of men?

Me mate, Davey, shuffles along the alleyway wall in front of us. He is a natural born leader. He stops turns and smiles as though reading my crazy thoughts. Man, his smile, it's a heartbreaker! It lights up his dark brown eyes and has broken many a girl's heart.

When we first arrived in Afghanistan the heat didn't seem to affect him. "It's my black heritage," he joked. "I knew it would come in handy someday, Mikey."

Today the heat is getting to him just as much as the rest of us. Lines of fatigue mark his face. Turning to me, he mouths, "Okay, Mikey?"

I lift me hand to acknowledge him and then turn to signal 'all clear' to the others covering me rear. With a sharp nod of his head Davey turns back, glancing from side to side, as he focuses on our surroundings to keep us moving forward.

Davey and me grew up together though he's a year and half older than me. Some say we're more like brothers than mates. That's true enough. Though not having a brother of me own I can't make a comparison. It has only ever been me and mum. I'm not even sure who me Dad is. Not that it matters.

I once tried questioning me Mum. She told me he wasn't even worth the price of the ticket that took him back to wherever it was he came from. So I didn't bother asking again.

Davey and me never attended a fancy school or had further education to teach us the finer things in life. Davey's mum always said her son was in a class of his own. We learnt about life the hard way growing up on a run-down housing estate in the inner city.

Under the bypass among the burnt-out cars and the windswept rubbish where the homeless made their homes, between the shit and discarded junkie needles, we would run and play. We learnt quickly to recognise friend from foe while watching, running and hiding as drug deals went down. We thought ourselves the lucky ones. Our hard working mums gave us a clean home, good home-cooked meals and fresh sheets to sleep between.

After leaving school with no qualifications, we were stuck doing the same dead end job and even shagging the same girl. Not that she minded. After all it wasn't as though we were ruining her career prospects.

Davey's Mum suggested to mine that it would do us both some good doing a stint in the army. At least it would get us away from the shit hole we were in after getting ourselves into a bit of bovver. I can still see our mums standing proudly together, both dressed in their finery, wanting us to be as proud of them as they were of us at our passing out parade.

I brush the flies away from me face gesturing to Davey that we're all accounted for and ready to move on his signal. I turn back confirming with Jimmy that everyone is good to go as he checks our rear. In front I see Davey step from view into one of the side alleys. A sudden burst of gunfire releases the hell that had been waiting in the shadows. It explodes onto the streets shattering the deafening silence. Explosions erupt all around us. I hit the ground with a thud amazed that our training has come into play.

Looking back over my shoulder I see Jimmy moving rapidly on his belly towards me his eyes showing me his dead man's vacant look.

"Where are the fucking little bastards this time?" he yells.

"How the fuck should I know!" I call, trying to locate where the shots are coming from.

"Where the fuck is Davey?"

"Up ahead somewhere. We'll have to get off this bloody street before we're dead men."

"We can't have you heading home in a black bag and gift wrapped," Jimmy shouts, as he puts his shoulder to a boarded-up doorway.

I scrutinize the rooftops, looking for the tell-tale signs of snipers. The door seems unforgiving as Jimmy shoulders it once again. Suddenly it bursts open and we tumble in followed by more rapid gunfire.

The airless space envelops us in a choking dust as the gunfire slices through the roof making us sitting ducks. Together Jimmy and I kick the back door open. We drop to our knees pressing our bodies against the wall. I glance around realising the alleyway is the one I saw Davey turn into earlier on.

"Where's the fucking back up?" Jimmy snarls. "Pissing hell the cavalry is never around when you need them."

As we inch our way along a narrow alley I abruptly stop, causing Jimmy to collide with me.

"What the fuck?"

"I don't know." I try to make sense of the upturned vegetable stalls and spilled produce. In the sweltering heat a chill runs through me as though an icy hand has closed around me heart. Among the discarded root vegetables and fruits, a pool of freshly spilled blood looked strangely out of place, making me skin crawl.

As I moved closer to take a better look I heard Jimmy cursing. "You're fucking mad, Mikey! I should shoot you now and save them the trouble. Where the fuck is Davey?"

"Shut the fuck up!" Me attention is on two distinct marks in the dirt. Me mind is telling me something. It screams louder than the explosions all around us. Suddenly, I understand that someone has dragged something. I'm aware of what I'm looking at, but me mind won't acknowledge it. I use the brightly coloured canopy of the upturned stall as protection, though I know it's useless. I edge me way round the enclosed space.

A shot rings out closely followed by a thud.

I glance over me shoulder and see Jimmy slumped against the wall.

57

"Shit, shit, shit." The words rattle from me like the sounds of the gunfire that rings in me ears.

I move slowly trying to focus on the green tarpaulin lying in a heap in the far corner of the square. Fear screams at me to get the hell out of there, but I need to know. I step forward using the tip of me gun to prod it. Unsure of what to do next, I hesitate. Stepping back, I hear a soft moan. I look over to where Jimmy lies half leaning against the bullet-shattered wall. There's a trickle of deep red blood spilling across the dusty alleyway.

Out of the corner of me eye I'm sure I see the tarpaulin move slightly. Then horror grips me heart as I catch a glimpse of a ring on a finger half exposed now.

I hold me breath and grab the tarpaulin. In one fluid movement I lift the sheet off. Beads of sweat trickle down me face as the sight that meets me eyes makes me inhale sharply.

"Your time to die now, pig!"

Somehow the tone of the voice doesn't go with the image before me. I'm staring down the barrel of a gun held by a child of about five. She squats on Davey's body grasping the gun with both of her small hands.

Davey's head rests amongst the discarded fruit and vegetable boxes but at a strange angle. His eyes stare up at me, open, in bewilderment. In the centre of his forehead, an unnatural hole spoils the once handsome, laughing face.

"You are a dirty pig. All American and British pigs must die," she squawks.

Her lips thin into a devilish smile. She raises the gun. I stare in horror into the black eyes and watch as her hands slowly tighten around the unwavering gun. Panic freezes me as me mouth dries. No amount of training has prepared me for this moment.

Suddenly the unnatural silence between us shatters as a

gun discharges. It deafens me and I close me eyes waiting for the pain of the bullet to pass through me. When it doesn't come, I open me eyes.

The child has disappeared and in her place lays a dwarfish woman. Thrown back over Davey's legs she lies with her arms outstretched as though in the sign of the cross. The top of her head is missing and her black eyes are closed forever.

"Hey Mikey don't let the fuckers screw with your mind." Jimmy clutches his side as his gun slips from his bloodied fingers.

Two days later I'm back on Civvy Street and heading home. I know I'll never be free from 'The War on Terror'. It haunts me day and night. I hear me brothers-in-arms calling to me, whilst watching me back. As I turn the corner and run up the flight of stairs I know there'll be two pairs of open arms waiting patiently to welcome me home. Their hearts broken like mine that our Davey didn't make it too.

Shadow Clock

At the age of twelve, while Hitler's bombs rained down on London, I learnt more about life as my granny lay dying. After a solicitor read her will Mother and I boarded a train with all our possessions including Granny's coffin as we then headed north. In the dimly-lit carriage Mother sat with her eyes closed, her face marred with tiredness, although I knew she wasn't sleeping.

"Mother?"

"Yes Jonathan." She opened her eyes. "Are you all right? Not too cold?"

"I'm fine. Does Father know where we're going?"

"Oh of course. Granny's solicitor, Mr Cutts, kindly forwarded a letter to Father's army headquarters. I've tried to keep him updated. Where we're going has a large garden. Won't that be grand to be self-sufficient in fresh fruit, vegetables and eggs?"

"We'll be keeping chickens then?"

"Yes once we've settled in. But there'll be lots to do first. The house has stood empty for a long time."

"Will Father recognise me when he comes home?"

"Of course, my dearest, why shouldn't he?"

"He's been away for such a long time."

The week before we left London, we'd sat at Granny's bedside chatting about the destruction of our city. On the odd occasion she'd nodded in an effort to join in, but most of the time she didn't seem to notice that we were even there.

Her head rested on the fluffy pillows. Her sunken features and watery blue eyes seemed void of life. Her thin, veiny hands lay unmoving on the crisp white sheets. Then one afternoon we arrived to find her sitting up in bed, looking years younger, with her hair cascading around her shoulders. Her eyes, though watery still, were full of life.

"My darling dears I've been worried that I might've missed you," she said.

"Deirdre you look amazing." Mother took her hand.

"Please sit, Ruth. I've something important to tell you. Firstly Jonathan this is for you." Granny held out a book. *The Magical Land of Noonday.*

When I was small she often read to me from it. At twelve I felt I had outgrown such stories.

"It's important that you look after the book," she said. "You're the keeper of the Noonday now."

A little confused, I glanced at Mother. She gave a slight nod.

"Granny I'm a little too old for such a book." However I took it, whilst noticing the cover showed the two children playing with their go-kart.

"Oh dear I should have spoken to you sooner." Granny turned to Mother. "Ruthie, please pass me my bag."

Mother placed the carpetbag with its tapestry flowers and a sundial on a woollen wall on Granny's lap. Granny produced a bunch of keys and selected a tiny gold one. With difficulty she stabbed repeatedly at the top of the bag until finally she inserted the key. It sprang open with an echoing click which neither Mother nor Granny noticed but it left a ringing in my ears. Granny thrust her hand in. A glow poured out lighting up hers and Mother's face in a golden aura. Again they didn't notice. Puzzled, I turned the book over and found that the cover now depicted a shadow clock like the one stitched on Granny's bag. "Granny, am I the keeper of the Noonday clock, like the one on your bag?" I held up the book.

"Please Jonathan, there's not much time. I need to tell—" Granny sunk back on her pillows, the freshness in her face faded. "Ruth, take the bag, keys, and the documents within. I have no need of them. I should've spoken to you – much sooner—"

Her breathing quickened as she spoke. Her lips transformed into thin blue lines. "Please, promise me you'll take them, Ruth."

"Oh Deirdre of course. I promise." Mother sobbed. "I'm sorry that John is not here."

"All's forgiven. Return the bag to my cottage. Take the letter to Mr Cutts. He'll know – foolish old woman, I... should've spoken sooner. Jonathan needs the 'knowledge'. Please forgive me." Granny gripped Mother's hand.

"Deirdre what are you talking about?"

"Speak to Mr Cutts. Wait at the cottage for John's return. Jonathan is needed there but be careful. Trust no one and nothing." Granny's voice faded, as her eyes closed.

"You mustn't worry, Deirdre. Now rest."

I took hold of Mother's hand.

"It's okay, Jonathan. Dying is as natural as living," she whispered, resting her head on my shoulder.

"What did Granny mean about me being the 'Keeper of the Noonday'?"

"You're the new owner of the book, I suppose."

Granny gave a rattling cough and turned her eyes on me. Her lips moved but formed no sounds. Suddenly her eyes widened and her body shook violently, lifting her from the bed.

Mother let out a gasp.

"Mother!" I exclaimed. A pain tore through my heart as the room plunged into darkness.

"Jonathan! What's wrong, son?" Mother's pleading voice came from afar.

An intense pain tore my head in half making it difficult for me to breathe. Then I heard Granny's voice.

"Relax Jonathan, you're safe. I'm with you always."

A rush of air filled my lungs and the tension left me. I drew in long deep breaths and the room came back into focus. "What happened?" I sobbed.

"Are you okay, Jonathan?"

"I think so." On retrieving the book I noticed that the clock on the cover showed four o'clock instead of midday – the same as my wristwatch. "Why does the cover keep—?"

"Oh Deirdre." Mother sat sobbing as tears streamed down her cheeks. She pulled me to her. My questions seemed unimportant as I tried to comfort her.

Mother and I sat in silence on the bus home. Suddenly the chatter around us melted away replaced by a wailing siren followed by a deafening boom that made the ground beneath the bus shudder. The bus skidded to a halt. "Everyone off now!" the driver yelled.

Some passengers cursed Hitler and his blessed bombs as we all gathered on the pavement unsure of what to do next. When a cloud of dust descended upon us making it hard to breathe, the driver hollered, "Get out of here!"

Mother and I pulled our scarves over our mouths and hurried home. On turning into our road we were confronted by a massive hole and piles of rubble.

"Oh dear Lord," Mother muttered.

In the unnatural silence through the dust I thought I heard the words, "shadow clock," but everyone was busy digging amongst the wreckage and looking for their loved ones. They stopped occasionally, crying out familiar names, before continuing to search. Mother put her arm around me. "We're leaving Jonathan. As soon as we've seen what's left of our house. We'll go straight to Mr Cutts."

"You can't come through here. It's too dangerous!" A man, covered in a layer of white dust, shouted at us as we picked our way over the wreckage of the homes.

"I'm sorry but we need to get to our house," Mother called.

"Hang on. Your house?" He moved ghost-like towards us.

"Yes." Mother pointed to the only remaining intact house. Even the sundial in the front garden seemed untouched by the bomb blast.

The man wiped his face. Tears streaked his dusty cheeks. "It's a bloody miracle, that is. Just be careful. Pack a bag fast and leave."

"Yes of course we will." Mother said.

We both expected the worst as Mother unlocked the door. The interior, like the front garden, hadn't a speck of dust anywhere. Plates, pictures and books all remained in their places. Mother ignored the man's advice. We took our time crating up our belongings and then sorted out Granny's coffin, before departing north a week later.

On the train I grew tired of watching the constantly changing landscape and reached for my duffel bag. Mother sat with her eyes closed.

"Are you okay?" I asked, even though I knew it was a daft question.

"Just a little concerned about what we'll find once we arrive. Mr Cutts said to expect the worst." Mother gave a light laugh.

On the cover of Granny's book a boy sat reading under the shadow clock. Another boy stood in a doorway pointing to a castle. "Maybe it's a kind of an adventure."

"You're right, Jonathan. It is an adventure."

"I meant—" I said, holding the book up but she cut me off.

"You read your book," she said closing her eyes. "I'll rest for a while."

The train raced on. Sunshine filled the carriage until the rain overtook us again as we pulled into the next station.

"Are we nearly there yet?" I asked, watching the passengers.

Mother lowered her book. "At least another three hours."

"Three hours." I tried to lower the window.

"Please leave it alone, Jonathan," Mother said tapping my legs with her book. "I don't want our carriage full of smoke."

"I can't see what's happening."

"They're taking on water, or coal. Do sit down."

I flopped into my seat and snatched up the book. The cover showed the boys on a cliff staring out to sea. In the distance a pirate ship sailed towards shore.

Was the book trying to warn me of impending danger? I flicked through some pages, but found to my disappointment that the contents hadn't changed. I tossed the book aside again.

Weary of sitting, and wanting to explore the other carriages, I knew Mother wouldn't allow it. "I need the toilet."

Mother lowered her book. "If you do Jonathan, don't get off the train."

I dashed along the corridor passing sleeping passengers. Many were Forces men and women. On reaching the lavatory door I glanced out of the window. In the shadows two soldiers lingered near the ticket office. Their animated gestures made me wonder whether they weren't sure if they had the right train or not.

The sudden call of nature made me hastily close the door behind me. I was back in our carriage by the time the train gave a shudder and let out a long whistle. I flung myself into my seat. Through a stream of smoke I caught sight of the two soldiers running along the platform; with an almost flying leap they caught our train.

Metallic boot studs echoed in the corridor outside our carriage as I opened my book. The next moment the door slid open and a young man, with a square face smiled in at us. "May we join you?"

"Please do," said Mother.

They tossed their bags onto the luggage rack and sat down. One of the soldiers scrutinized my book and grinned as he said, "I always loved those stories when I was young."

I ignored him and focused on the racing landscape beyond the window. The rain-filled sky reflected the carriage interior. *Something looked different* – I studied it for a moment and then gasped. Not quite believing what I saw. There was a change in what the two soldiers now wore. Was the reflection in the glass showing me them in their true form? I was sure it was, but how I didn't know.

"Are you heading home or returning to camp?" Mother asked, as she opened the carpetbag and took out a small lunch box.

"Heading home. I'm Oswald Brand," the second soldier said. "He's Bane Haward."

"I'm Mrs Markham and he's my son, Jonathan. Pleased to meet you both. Would you care to join us for a bite to eat?"

"We're fine, thank you," Bane said. "Nice bag. Did you make it, Mrs Markham?"

"No, my mother-in-law did."

"Interesting design," Bane said, closing his eyes.

As the soldiers slept, Mother and I ate our sandwiches and read. On waking the soldiers chatted with Mother about the war. I went back to studying their reflections within the glass of the window. I saw some sort of aura shift between the two soldiers. It transformed their khaki uniforms into green velvet tunics. Under a surcoat they wore worked leather corset-like armour with heavy silver straps over well-padded shoulders. On the front of the armour was the insignia of an oak tree. Carved into the trunk of the tree was a shadow clock like the one on Granny's bag. The soldiers wore greenish-brown suede breeches and leather brown boots. The only place I had seen such a uniform was in my school history book of Anglo-Saxon Britain.

I turned away from the window. Within their highly polished black army boots I saw quite clearly the reflection of Mother and me. Yet somehow everything linked back to the shadow clock.

"Were you in France, by any chance?" Mother asked.

"Jonathan, wake up."

I rubbed my eyes and sat up. "Where are Bane and Oswald?"

"They left when we fell asleep, I suppose. Hurry otherwise we'll miss our connection." Mother handed me some luggage just as I went to take it my book fell to the floor. The boys now stood beside a church with a sundial.

"Jonathan put that book away," Mother snapped. "I need your help."

As we boarded our last train, I thought about Bane and Oswald. Was it possible I had dreamt them? "Mother did the soldiers know anything about Father?"

"Oh darling, France is a very big place. To be honest I was checking that they weren't spies."

"What made you think they were?"

"Nothing really. Though Bane seemed especially interested in Granny's bag. I would've hated to lose it when she insisted it was returned to the cottage."

"Why would they want it?

"No idea. He was just admiring the needlework. Nothing more.

"Are you sure they were British soldiers?"

"No one can be a hundred per-cent sure of anything. War has us all on edge."

I wanted to tell Mother what I had seen in the glass window, but somehow I wasn't even convinced myself that they were Anglo-Saxon warriors, so I thought better of it.

The train shuddered to a halt as we pulled into the station. An elderly stationmaster helped Mother down.

"Mrs Markham?"

"Yes."

"Terrible weather. We'll have you on your way soon."

The stationmaster gestured to a porter with a trolley to help unload the goods wagon. The three elderly men, dressed in tailcoats, doffed their top hats and lowered their eyes as they took possession of Granny's coffin. Mother and I waited with our belongings while the porter went to fetch a cart. With a nod, Mr Weatherill, the cart's owner, helped Mother up while I hopped into the back.

"Are thee comfortable, lad?" he asked.

"Yes Sir." I sat with my back against a wooden crate.

"Giddy up." Mr Weatherill said with a shake of the reins. With a jolt the cart horse set the cart in motion. "Ah'm so sorry to hear about dear old Mrs Markham's passing." The carter gave a light cough.

"So you knew my mother-in-law well?"

As Mother and Mr Weatherill chatted about Granny, I dozed.

When the cart hit a pothole I woke with a start. A steep slope rose before us. I willed the horse on.

"Thank you, Master Markham. So glad to have you back," a labouring voice said.

Had Mr Weatherill read my thoughts? I shook my head puzzled. I was sure I had dreamt it, as Mother and he were in deep conversation.

"Hang on tight," Mr Weatherill called over his shoulder and turned the cart off onto a track.

Finally after a rough ride up from the village Mr Weatherill halted the cart.

The cottage, a grey two-storey farmhouse, stood among ancient forest of gnarled trees which echoed to the cawing of rooks and crows. An air of neglect hung around everything with peeling paint, broken guttering and an overgrown garden.

"We're 'ere, young Mrs Markham," Mr Weatherill said, as heavy raindrops began to fall.

Mother jumped down and ran up the steps. "Please give me a moment before you start unloading!" She called over her shoulder. "I know you'll want to be getting home as soon as possible.

The porch had, above its archway, a unicorn with one leg raised carved in the stone. The solid oak door had, at its centre, a brass squirrel knocker and two thick ornate metal hinges like the ones I had seen on the shoulder straps of the warriors.

"It had to be the last key on the ring," Mother said.

We entered a narrow hallway and were hit by blast of stale air.

"Gosh it's dark in here. I hope we have electricity," Mother said, mirroring my thoughts.

"Help Mr Weatherill, Jonathan while I find the fuse box in the kitchen. Granny's letter said something about a generator but I won't know how to work it. Put everything in the front room for now."

Soon we had everything inside the house and Mr Weatherill was on his way home. Mother sorted out a couple of crates for what we needed straightaway. While she was in the kitchen, I hurried towards the stairs.

As I reached for the banister my hand brushed against

the ornate newel wooden post and a tingling sensation raced up my arm. In the fading light all I could see was some sort of carved procession going towards a church or maybe a castle.

"Jonathan, you can look later. These are heavy," Mother said, coming up behind me with an armful of blankets and sheets.

In the large front bedroom stood an unmade double bed, a dressing table, and wardrobe. At the windows were faded red velvet curtains. Mother plonked the bedding down on the mattress which sent up a cloud of dust which made us both cough.

"Oh dear," she said, struggling to breathe. "Open the windows."

I lifted the latch but the window wouldn't budge.

"It hasn't been opened for a while. Try pushing on the frame. I'll go and find what I need to clean the room before making the bed."

I put my shoulder to the window frame and pushed. It swung out almost taking me with it. As I struggled to pull myself in something brushed against my face followed by many chattering voices. "Freedom – we're free at last—"

In the fading light I saw nothing, just some flickering lights in the valley below.

"Be careful," Mother said. "Right you go and find yourself a bedroom and see if there's a bathroom up here too while I clean.

Next door was the bathroom Mother had hoped for, but what caught my attention was the door after it. As I reached for the acorn-shaped door handle I heard someone say, "He's here!"

I stopped myself from calling out to Mother. I told myself I needed to be brave with Father away. Gingerly I opened the door. In the half-light the room seemed to be full of ghostly shadows. They stood against the walls and crouched in the centre of the room.

"Jonathan."

My stomach lurched.

"Jonathan – I've found a couple of Tilley lamps."

The breath I'd held burst from me. As my curiosity deserted me, I dashed downstairs and erupted into the kitchen.

Mother turned with a metal jug in her hand. "For goodness sake don't charge about especially with lit paraffin lamps in the house.

"Sorry Mother."

"Have you found a bedroom?"

"I think so."

"Take this one. Be careful – the glass will get hot.

I carefully took the long handles pleased we had lighting."

The flickering flames of the lamp caused the shady creatures and figures on the newel post to dance towards the castle with their swords held high as we climbed the stairs.

"Is this the bedroom you've chosen?" Mother asked, pointing towards the open door.

"Yes." I hesitated. The room seemed to be waiting for me.

Mother walked straight in, threw open the curtains and opened the window. "Now pull off the dust sheets and shake them outside while I start to give the room a quick clean."

The ghosts disappeared along with the dust covers and cobwebs as the room was transformed into a light airy space.

"Did you notice the woods beyond the garden, Jonathan?"

"Yes," I muttered while eyeing the bed. It towered over me reminding me of a pirate ship but without its rigging. On the headboard a carved procession of people mirrored the one on the newel post, travelled up and over the ornate wooden canopy. I joined Mother at the window.

"Your father talked about a ruined castle somewhere hereabouts."

"Really. A castle?" All the negative thoughts about the headboard evaporated.

"He said he could see it from his bedroom window."

"I can't see anything but trees."

"Oh Jonathan," Mother laughed. "Your father lived here over thirty years ago. Anyway let's turn the mattress. I shall need your help."

Mother took her lamp and went to fetch more bedding. I moved my lamp towards the bookcase. The tension within the room shifted causing the shadows to dance across the walls. I ignored them and focused on the chest.

It had three curved metal straps over its domed lid. On the front, either side of a battered lock, were two hand-painted lozenges depicting garden scenes. One showed a fountain of a stone boy holding a shell. The other depicted a church with an arched doorway and a sundial above it.

I searched the room for a key after being unable to open the chest. The last place I had to look was the bottom drawer in the built-in wardrobe. I tugged at it but it was stiff. It moved a few inches giving me a large enough gap to squeeze my hand in. When my fingertips made contact with something soft and warm I gasped in surprise almost falling backwards. In the lamplight a pair of blinking black eyes stared at me.

"What are you doing?" Mother asked, placing her lamp on the chest of drawers.

I jumped up. "The drawer it's—"

"Jonathan, are you all right?"

"Hmm, yes—"

"Don't worry about that now." Mother lifted the chest lid easily. "Well Granny certainly knew how to keep things fresh and the moths out." Mother removed layers of tissue paper and dried lavender sticks scented the bedroom. "Goodness, what a brightly coloured quilt." Mother said, pulling it out of the chest. As we straightened the quilt on the freshly made bed my stomach tightened. I thought I heard a scratching noise coming from the drawer in the wardrobe.

"I'm not sure we've put the quilt on the right way round," Mother said, pointing. "The house looks to be on upside down."

The centre panel depicted our house in various shades of grey, green and red fabrics. The porch was there with its unicorn, its one leg raised as though pointing to something.

I leant over the bed. "Oh look there's the castle and a squirrel with a gold nut."

"It's beautifully detailed," Mother said. "Let's have something to eat. In the morning, you can have a good look while you're making the bed. I expect you to keep your room tidy."

The sunlight pouring through the gap in the curtains woke me. With excitement I leapt out of bed and pulled the curtains back. I studied the detailed carving on the headboard. It depicted a castle with a large tree within its walls. An array of birds perched in the top branches of the tree while on its trunk a squirrel ran and at its base, laid a cave, in which a dragon slept with seven knights.

The quilt, I soon realised, was a map. The unicorn's leg was actually pointing towards the castle. I leapt off the bed pulled on my clothes and dashed for the stairs.

Light flooded the landing from the open door giving life

to the carved figures on the newel post making me pause in my rush to get outside. Two small boys seemed to be leading a band of men and dwarves towards a castle while in the distance ships were coming ashore. I recalled that Granny's book had a similar cover. Downstairs, I pushed the kitchen door open. Mother had been busy as I was met by a brightly-lit room.

"Good morning, Jonathan. Did you sleep well?" she asked, turning with a saucepan in hand.

"Yes I did and you?"

"Very much so. It's so peaceful here. I can't believe we're at war. I left the range alight during the night so there's hot water now. Once I'm familiar with it I'll start baking bread again. For now there's only porridge." Mother placed a bowl in front of me.

I feared my breakfast would taste of death as it came from London. I lifted a spoonful to my lips and sniffed it first.

"Is everything all right?" she asked, taking the seat opposite me.

"Yes," I swallowed. To my delight it tasted creamy.

Mother ate some of hers before saying, "First I need to speak to the undertakers. Afterwards we'll go shopping."

"Can I go hunting for the castle this morning?" I asked, pushing my empty bowl away.

"No. There's too much to do. I've no idea how many guests to expect for Granny's wake. Mr Weatherill said she was well-known in these parts." In a softer tone she added, "I'm sorry, Jonathan but I really do need your help."

"I know."

On returning to my bedroom to collect my shoes I glimpsed the view of the woods. It was clearer now. The sunlight heightened the shadows making the steep path easily identifiable as it wound its way from the edge of our garden up through the trees. I sighed disappointed that I couldn't explore. I pulled Father's old binoculars from my bag and zoomed in.

In among the dried grasses and weeds at the bottom of our garden a statue of a boy, holding a seashell, came into view. It was identical to the one on the chest. Was it possible that the illustrations on the book cover, the chest and the carvings around the house were linked to real life?

I went to the landing. Below Mother was busy in the kitchen. I investigated a small door I had seen on my way downstairs. Carved into the door was a face surrounded by foliage. I tried to find a means of opening it. There, hidden by the wooden foliage, was a small sunken brass ring and keyhole.

I fetched Granny's key ring from Mother's room. On finding the right one it gave a satisfying click. I pulled the door open and stood back. When nothing happened I leaned into the darkness waiting for my eyes to adjust. An indistinct sound made me turn. I expected to see Mother coming upstairs and I almost fell over backwards when something furry brushed against my arm; russet-brown in colour it disappeared into my bedroom. I froze unsure of what it was.

Gathering courage I went to check. There was nothing but my shoes under the bed. I lit the lamp and carried it to the doorway.

The lamplight revealed a set of well-worn, wooden steps curving upwards into the roof. Huge cobwebs danced in the shadows as I climbed the stairs. The air, though musty, had a peculiar smell.

At the top the space opened out. Shapes leapt out at me. Shelves full of dusty books, rows of jars and candlesticks; whilst overhead a rack with dry plants and cobwebs hung from a beam.

In one corner a broken roof tile allowed a shaft of light to enter. I picked up a large wooden spoon and prodded the rain-soaked mess on the floor, and realised it had once been a book.

Under the wet paper was a rusty biscuit tin. I gave it a shake and something within clunked. I prised it open.

The moon's silvery leet creates shadows across the floor. Ah fear no evil. Mi heart hears the call of the wild, but at night, it is the strongest.

As I read on the words became familiar to me.

Ah'm Jonah of twelve summers past. Pa says Ah must swear mi allegiance to King Edward but Ah wish to devote mi life to another calling. Since Granny Markham became aware that Ah understood more than most she's been teaching me the knowledge from the book of Grimoire.

For she, like me, understands all creatures. In mi mind Ah follow the flight of the ullets, the barn and tawny, the boggart and the king on their nightly hunts along the edges of the fields and among the trees. Within mi heart Ah see what they see and taste their freedom.

When tomorrow comes Pa will be disappointed that Ah cannot kill the wild creatures that speak so freely to me.

Below Ah hear voices but its neither Pa nor Ma. Ah sensed the boy's uneasiness, he's like me, but is unaware. Ah cross to the door ready to welcome mi descendants into mi home.

"Jonathan Markham! What are you doing?"
I lowered the book. "Sorry Mother,"
"Didn't you hear me calling?" She tugged at an old sack

above her head. It came away with ease and with it a shower of dust. A burst of sunlight through a skylight briefly blinded us as we started coughing.

"Gosh this is an amazing space." Mother forgot her annoyance and crossed to the fireplace. "Look at these books."

She plucked one from the shelf and flicked a few pages. "These are old. This one seems to be written in Latin. I wasn't aware Granny understood Latin. Have you noticed the strange symbols carved on the outer doors and on the stonework? Her fingertips traced the stone face on the mantelpiece," I thought they were to protect the house from witches but who knows?"

"Why not look them up in one of your books?" I asked. My mind still on what I had just read.

"Of course. How silly of me to not practice what I preach. Once I've had a good look at these," she tapped the book spines, "I might find enough room up here for my own. What are you reading?" She held out her hand.

"A book."

"I can see it's a book, silly." She gave a light laugh.

Reluctantly I passed it over.

"It's written by a competent hand. With all the Ah and Ullet for owls. Whoever Jonah was, he was a local. The Yorkshire dialect is as close to olde English as you can get."

"I found it there." I pointed to the corner. "The rain's getting in."

"We can't have that," Mother said leaning against the wall and looking up. "Let's just hope it hasn't been like it for too long. Why wasn't the book damaged?"

"It was wrapped up." I held up a funny sort of cloth.

"Oilskin," she said hardly taking her eyes from the page. "I wonder if the symbols around the house are somehow linked to this." Mother showed me a page full of

77

doodles. They looked the same as the symbols on the quilt, bed and the newel post. "After Granny's funeral I'll unpack my books. We can have some fun making pencil rubbings of the symbols around the house and looking them up together."

I rewrapped the book placing it in the tin and set it out of harm's way.

"Now please get ready, Jonathan and don't take too long this time," she said, locking the door behind us.

A few minutes later I heard Mother shouting, "Jonathan, are you ready?"

"Just looking for my shoes!" I yelled back, crawling under the bed trying to find them. As I reached out my fingertips touched something hard. On pulling it out I discovered, not my shoe, but a wooden squirrel. In its front paws it held a golden hazelnut.

"Cor, you're a beauty." I placed it on the floor and continued hunting for my shoes.

"Please Jonathan! Come on."

"I'm just looking for my other shoe."

"Don't make me come up, Jonathan."

I began searching the room again, only to discover that the wooden squirrel had disappeared and in its place was my missing shoe.

"Jonathan?"

"I'm coming." I pulled on my shoes, but as I put my left foot down a pain shot up my leg. I tore off the shoe and tipped it up. In the palm of my hand there rested a golden nut.

"Now Jonathan!"

After the heavy rain the track to the village was muddy. As I followed Mother I pondered on how the golden hazelnut had got into my shoe. The wooden squirrel had been real. Well in as much as a wooden squirrel could be

78

real. In my pocket my fingertips explored the surface of the nut. I wanted to take it out and have a good look but I needed to keep up with Mother.

Mother pointed to a footpath sign. "I think we should see where it goes."

The path descended through wet bracken and gave us a wonderful view across the valley.

"Look there's a market on today." Mother pointed towards the centre of the village. "Now that's a bit of luck." Situated alongside the undertakers we found a baker, butchers and a hardware store with a garage. "Right I won't be long. While I sort out Friday's arrangements you can see what's available."

After a quick look around I returned to the market stall next to the undertakers. The stall sold caged birds, vegetables and jars of preserves. Four ruddy-brown hens sat in a small cage.

The stall holder, a sturdy farmer, studied me closely from under his tweed cap. He only looked away when Mother appeared at my side.

"Jonathan we need to visit the church next. It isn't far."

"Look Mother – chickens. Can we buy them?"

Mother knelt before the cage. "They do look healthy but I'm not sure whether we've anywhere to keep them. And we'll need food too."

"Are thee Mrs Markham's grandson?" The farmer said, removing his cap and offering me his hand.

I took his rough, calloused hand. "I am."

"Then it is mighty fine to meet thy mother and thee. I'm Jack Bullett. My farm th' 'ther side o' Shadow Clock house."

"So you're our nearest neighbour?" Mother asked.

"That Ah'll be. Will thee be interested in th' hens?"

"Very much so – as fresh eggs would be lovely, but with

a funeral on Friday I haven't the time to find somewhere secure in the garden to keep them safe. The garden is very overgrown at the moment."

"Old Mrs Markham has a hen house. Ah'll tell thee what Ah'll bring them over later. Ah've some feed too though they'll also scratch about the garden. Just need shutting up at night otherwise Foxy'll get them."

"Thank you, Mr Bullett. Please let me pay for them and the few other bits too. It'll save me carrying them to the church," Mother said, opening her purse. We headed out on the old drove road to the Kirk on the outskirts of the village.

"We must've missed the entrance," Mother said as we found ourselves on a grassy track. "Mr Bullett did warn us it was well hidden."

We backtracked. At the bottom of a slope a square-towered church with a large porch, which mirrored the one on our house, sat nestled within a wooded bank.

"What a lovely building," Mother said. "It's early Anglo-Saxon – though the tower looks to be nineteenth century, and the porch Norman."

The church door burst open just as we entered the porch. A tall, thin man with a bluff, jovial visage, dressed in a cassock, hurried out carrying a pile of books.

"Oh my –I wasn't expecting—" He left his sentence unfinished as the door banged shut behind him. "So sorry – Hello may I help?"

"Good afternoon. I'm Mrs Markham. I'm looking for the rectory."

"Mrs Markham I wasn't expecting you so soon. I'm the Reverend Charles Girth. Please come this way," He led us around the back of the church. "My wife knew your mother-in-law well. I think a nice cup of tea is in order."

"Oh did she? Tea would be lovely. Could my son look around the church while we chat?"

"But of course. He can join us afterwards for tea and cakes. My grandson will be over later. It would be good for the two boys to get to know each other, Mrs Markham. Right see that footpath there?" He pointed to a small gate half hidden by gravestones. "It goes straight to the rectory. Err?"

"Jonathan sir."

"Please take your time, Jonathan. There's a lot to see. Two amazing tombstones."

In the graveyard there were a few stones with our family's names on but that was all. Next I investigated the porch. On either side of the door stood two stone slabs engraved with a cross. Above the door in the centre of a stone slab, was a shadow clock. Engraved around the clock were the words, '*Haward wrought me and Brand, the Prior*'.

"Gosh, those were the names of the two soldiers on the train." I said aloud.

On entering the church the door slammed behind me with an echoing bang. As the sound died away a sense of peace floated around the lofty, pale interior with its high Saxon arches and simple wooden plaques. I looked at its ancient font and the colourful stained glass windows, but what caught my attention were the two Saxon gravestones. I wondered who lay beneath the carved strap-work and circles. Behind the high altar I saw a decorative wooden panel, depicting the same design as the one on my bed, with the hidden face among the wooden foliage.

"The Green Man – the church and house are linked." I continued to say my thoughts aloud.

A squirrel, caught in mid-action, ran along the tree trunk with a golden nut in its mouth. I pulled the hazelnut from my pocket and held it against the one the squirrel grasped. As the two touched a flash of light blinded me. In its brightness an image of a man trapped in a dark place appeared.

81

The man seemed somehow familiar but the sound of voices echoing around the church broke my concentration. I dropped to my knees and hid under the high altar cloth, fearing that I was somewhere where I shouldn't be.

Though what the voices were saying was indistinguishable they were familiar to me. They weren't Mother's or the vicar's. I was hunched in an uncomfortable position and I tried to stretch my legs. I put my hand out to get some leverage and to my horror it came in contact with a pair of beaten leather boots. The cloth lifted and I looked into the eyes of Bane Haward.

"Greetings Master Markham. Ah can assure thee we're not thy enemies though it's good thou have sought sanctuary." He held his hand out to me. As I took it and he pulled me up. Bane wasn't dressed in Army khakis now instead he was dressed as a Saxon warrior.

"Sanctuary? No my mother came to talk to the vicar about—" I stopped. What had happened to the church's interior? The pews, flowers, wall plaques and the gravestones were gone. Only the high altar and a few wall paintings remained.

"Come there's much to do, Master Markham." Bane interrupted my thoughts.

Outside everything looked different too. The tower and porch had gone, leaving the shadow clock exposed. Now the sun marked the passing of time.

"Has time turned back?" I asked.

"When these shores are under attack everyone must do their duty," Bane said, as he strode off, leaving me staring at an empty graveyard apart from a few wooden markers.

"Have the Germans landed?" I asked, running to catch him up.

"Ships are heading towards our shore. We must join Oswald and the others along the coast."

"How did I get here?" I reached for my pocket and

found it was missing. I looked down and discovered I wore a tunic and breeches. "Oh no I've lost the nut." To my relief, I found a soft leather pouch hanging from a thin belt at my waist. I opened it and found the nut nestled inside among a few odd shaped silver and gold coins. I picked one out. It was thick on one side, thin on the other and at its centre was stamped a picture of a sun.

I caught up with Bane as he surveyed a rutted dirt track, that a short time ago had been a tarmac one; the one which Mother and I had arrived upon.

"Thou came to the church looking for help?" Bane said, dropping to his knees and pressing his hand against the ground.

"No I came to see the vicar," I said, curious as to what Bane was doing.

"Thou asked for our help to drive out the invaders?"

"The Germans you mean?"

"We must hurry."

A low whistle filled the air.

"What was that?"

"'Tis a warning not to dither, Master Markham." Bane dragged me into the undergrowth. "Danger is coming. Keep moving."

Without protest I followed.

Suddenly Bane yanked me to the ground as a thunderous sound filled the air.

"What's happening?" I peered over the log. In the dappled sunlight a parade of flowing capes, knee-length mail-shirts and a flashing of metal, as five horsemen rode ahead of a wagon, pulled by two white oxen.

"Who are they?"

"Norman soldiers." Bane pulled me further down. "We can't afford to be caught by them."

"Why is the man blindfolded?"

"That be Jonah's father. Follow me."

"Jonah?" I said surprised to hear the name I read in the book I found in the attic.

"All will be explained. A man's life is at stake."

In a clearing a brown horse stood patiently. Bane patted its rump. It turned its large head and nodded.

"Please allow me to introduce Redwold. The finest horse thou art likely to meet. And he knows it too." Bane gave a laugh and tugged the reins free from a tree. He leapt onto its back and then pulled me up behind him. With a light kick, we were off.

"Hang on tight, Master Markham." A voice unlike Bane's said.

I looked around.

"'Tis I, Redwold. Named after a great king thou knowth."

"But you're a horse?"

"I am. Are you not aware of your powers? You hear and understand all living creatures? Oh hang on tight, Master Markham."

I clung to Bane's cloak as the strength of Redwold vibrated through my legs. Was I dreaming? I pressed hard against Bane's back finding reassurance in the smell of his sweat.

Soon we began to climb. Between the tall trees I caught glimpses of a castle. As the path levelled out in the distance the sea and sky appeared to become one. Bane turned Redwold onto a less-trodden path. On entering the forest we had to bend low to avoid the branches. The trees were full of chattering birds and overhead I heard the pitiful calls of the buzzards. Soon I heard the voices of men.

In a clearing we passed a cluster of wooden shelters, their thatched roofs mottled in the dappled light, while chickens pecked at the ground. In the doorways two slender young women, dressed in long gowns, stood with babies on their hips, watching us with interest. A delicious smell filled the air making my stomach rumble. As we approached a group of warriors seated on logs round a smoking fire pit, one of them suddenly leapt up and with a grunt drew his sword. Instantaneously the others joined him, until only one remained seated Bane jumped down from his horse as Oswald stood to greet him with a bear hug. The warriors lowered their swords as Oswald said, "Welcome. Ah hope thou's brought us mead and good news, my dear friends. Ah Master Markham, we've been waiting for your arrival. Come, time to eat." I sat where he gestured.

Hungry men eagerly leant forward. One of the warriors used his sword to clear away the hot ashes off the fire pit. A burst of flames lit up their scarred, grubby faces. The warrior stabbed a cooked chicken, fat dripping from it, as he passed it to the nearest man. Unflinching, the man ripped the bird in half and shared it with Bane and I.

After the meal Bane began to explain what we had seen. As tempers rose my bladder tightened. I looked for somewhere to relieve myself. Bane seemed to sense my need and nodded in the direction of a thicket. "Be careful. Don't get lost."

I dashed for the woods. Under a hanging rock a clear pool bubbled. After relieving myself I knelt to wash my hands and face. On straightening I saw two reflections within the water; both were mine. I drew myself up careful to keep my hands in sight so he knew I carried no weapons. Though the boy looked like me, his hair was longer.

"Who are you?" I already knew the answer.

"Ah's Jonah Markham. Thee be Jonathan, so Bane tells me."

A movement in the branches above his head caught my

attention. A flash of red dropped onto his shoulder. Jonah turned his head slightly as a squirrel chatted into his ear.

"Oh so thou have met Jonathan already?"

"Met?" I asked unable to comprehend the squirrel's chatter.

The squirrel flicked its tail and sprung noisily from Jonah's shoulder back into the branches.

"Ratatosk tells me thee has something of his."

"Oh the nut," I said, as my hand went to the purse. I was about to show Jonah when he grabbed my arm and raised his finger to his lips.

"We need to leave now," he whispered, as the sound of marching feet moved in our direction.

Back at the encampment the newcomers chatted among themselves until Bane rode into the centre of them. The growing mass of warriors came in all shapes and sizes and reminded me of the procession carved into the newel post and bed. As Bane began to speak the men's voices faded away.

"Thank you for answering our call-to-arms, brothers. We must fight against the evil that invades our land. We must take back the castle before nightfall." The warriors raised their swords and with whooping and hollering they climbed on their horses and ponies.

"Come lad," Bane said pulling me up behind him as Jonah mounted his own horse.

Our numbers grew the closer we got to the castle. On entering a clearing we came under attack. I clung to Bane's cloak the best I could as he swung his sword striking the Norman soldiers.

Amid the clashing of metal and screams, without warning Redwold reared up. Everything spiralled in a haze of horses and men's legs as I landed with a thud in the mud, blood and guts.

Surrounded by the clangour of swords and an endless dance of horses' hooves and soldiers' feet, I crawled, while trying to dodge dead and dying men.

"Get to thy feet!"

Jonah's voice floated through the carnage as I fought my way through the wheezing men. They wielded their swords as their horses snorted in terror. "Get out of here!" Bane shouted. I reached Jonah.

"Follow me," Jonah said, pulling my arm.

From nowhere a Norman soldier appeared, wielding a double attack. Bane jumped from Redwold. He parried with a sword and dagger as the Norman lunged at him. Bane lifted his sword in an effort to get a clear swing. I saw the lines of tiredness mark Bane's face as he battled on. One wrong move and he would die.

Around us shouts and screams echoed as Jonah pulled me into a dark tunnel. I retched as the smell hit me. It clawed at the back of my throat. I stuck out my hand to steady myself and made contact with something cold and slimy that clung to the walls. I let out a gasp.

"Hush, we need to open the gates before we lose too many men."

I stumbled after him trying not to think about what I was walking on. Soon the air became easier to breathe.

"We must go up." Jonah pointed to a hole. "Do exactly what Ah tell thee."

We moved slowly; our soft leather boots made no sound on the stone floor. Outside we could hear the arrows raining down on the men within the courtyard along with the constant screams and the endless clashing of metal against metal outside the castle's wall.

On the stone staircase over our heads we heard the clattering sound of panicked footfalls. Jonah burst into a sprint pulling me with him into a dimly-lit corridor.

"Quickly in here!" he lifted a tapestry. We flattened ourselves against the cold wall just as someone rushed by shouting. "They're attacking the southern gate!"

After a moment Jonah swept the wall hanging aside and said, "Now!"

We darted along the passage. At the end, Jonah peered round a corner. I glanced back, just in time to see a monk and a nun emerge from a room and hurry off in the opposite direction. Moments later a woman, dressed in a lavender-blue gown, emerged from the same place. For a second the woman's eyes locked onto mine. I thought she was going to sound the alarm but she just smiled at me. Something about her smile seemed so familiar. She turned and dashed after her companions. Jonah and I circled the windy courtyard avoiding flaming rags dipped in tar. Amid the chaos we reached the massive gate wheel housing. The rough wooden frame towered over us. Jonah's laboured breathing filtered through to me as he tried to pull while I pushed but the wheel refused to budge.

Looking up I saw the counter weight and gestured to Jonah's dagger. With a nod he handed it to me. I fastened it to my belt and began to climb the housing. The wood dug into my hands. Below flashes of sparks flew as metal clashed against metal. Arrows whizzed past me. I reached level with the weight and began cutting the rope.

Jonah's pale face stared up at me. I waved him aside as I cut through the rope. For a second I feared the spinning wheel would crush him as the weight dropped and the gate lifted.

With a rattling bang the gate rose. Bane and his warriors roared in their swords and axes slicing through the Normans in a shower of blood, bones and guts.

I climbed down so far and then jumped, crash-landing at Jonah's feet. He hauled me up and said, "This way."

As we ran I handed his dagger back. We darted between

the battling soldiers. Without warning I lost my footing and skidded through the blood, mud and burning rags. Powerless to stop myself I crashed into the body of a fallen soldier. As I struggled to my knees I came face to face with a pair of soulless eyes. I retched at the sight of grey matter spilling from the top of the soldier's head. In the flickering light I snatched a dagger from his chest and ran. I took the stone steps two at a time and descended into the darkness. I was ready to call out when a low chattering close by stopped me.

"Ratatosk is that you?"

A weight dropped onto my shoulder startling me. I stifled a cry and asked, "Where's Jonah?"

The squirrel leapt to the floor and scampered into the darkness chattering noisily. At an intersection he waited for me. Ahead I heard the faint sound of voices and saw a glow of light moving deeper into the dungeon. I advanced towards it, when a hand drew me back.

"Jonathan," Jonah whispered.

"Oh—"

"Hush it's too dangerous. Come."

Death scented the air. In the flickering torchlight skeletal men hung with their feet barely touching the filthy floor. Jonah tugged on my sleeve. Ahead the voices were louder now.

"Tell us who thou art working for?"

My stomach churned at the sound of a birch striking skin. An agonizing scream pierced the air. Jonah pointed, and we moved cautiously on. A noise behind us made me turn. Before I could alert Jonah a hand fell across my mouth.

"Hush Jonathan," a voice whispered.

"Oh Bane. They're hurting mi Pa," Jonah sobbed.

"Don't worry. We're here to free 'im."

The six warriors crept along the passage while Jonah and I followed. Suddenly a Norman soldier materialized before them. Without giving him a chance Oswald drove a dagger into his chest. The passage opened into a hellhole of torture. On some of the devices men hung dying. Jonah ignored the danger and raced past the torturers to the blood-soaked man hanging from a frame. I followed – dagger in hand.

The Norman soldiers charged at Bane and his warriors. As they fought, Jonah and I sawed through the ropes that bound his father. Jonah freed one arm and started on his leg. His father turned to me, "Thank you my son."

"I'm not your—"

"Look out, Jonathan!" Bane bellowed.

Dagger in hand I leapt driving it into a blood-soaked Norman's throat as he rose up behind Jonah. With a murmur he sank to the floor.

A groan burst from Bane. His sword clattered to the floor as his warning almost cost him his life. I rushed to his side as blood oozed from his arm. I cut my belt in half and tied it tight around the top of his arm.

"Our fight is done, Bane. Thou must return Jonathan to the church," Oswald said.

"What of Jonah's father?" I asked.

"We go now," Bane pleaded, through gritted teeth. "All is well with him now."

Supporting Bane we circled the dead and dying as Oswald brought Redwold to us. With difficulty Bane mounted and hauled me up behind him. "Thou are needed in thine own time."

"They won't believe me!"

"Thou must make them." He urged Redwold on.

In the fading light Bane's weight shifted in his struggle to remain upright. Whether Redwold understood the urgency or not he trotted along the path that skirted the woods until we arrived at the church. With a struggle Bane slipped off Redwold's back. I went to support him but he shook me off.

"Nee Lad. Fear not." He leant against a grave marker his blood seeping from under the tourniquet. "Thou must pass under the shadow clock before night returns."

Reluctantly I dashed towards the church just as a dark cloud moved across the sun. I shouldered the heavy oak door. It gave just as Bane slid to the ground. I gasped. Caught mid-motion I fell backwards as a burst of sun blinded me. The slamming of the door echoed around me as I opened my eyes. Sunlight streamed through the windows bathing everything in an array of ethereal colours. A pair of strong arms lifted me to my feet as I stared up into my grandmother's smiling face.

"Granny, you're... the lady in the lavender dress."

"Jonathan, listen. Your father needs your help."

"But he's abroad."

"No, he's imprisoned in the castle. The shadow clock has allowed you to gain the knowledge you needed by helping your ancestor, Jonah, to free his father. Now you've learnt the way in and where the hidden rooms are in the castle. You'll be able to help your father."

"Why is he here at the castle?"

"He's part of the Resistance and works undercover for the British Government. His job was to infiltrate the Nazis, but his cover was blown."

"Like Jonah's father?"

"Yes, history repeated itself. Be quick, for your father's sake."

She stepped forward. I closed my eyes ready for her embrace, inhaling the sweet smell of lavender. When her warmth never came, I opened my eyes and she was gone.

I burst into the rectory, calling, "Mother! They're at the castle!"

"Jonathan, what is it?" Mother appeared. Panic lined her face. "Who's at the castle?"

"Spies! I saw them."

"Spies?"

Reverend Girth appeared. "Spies? I do hope you're not fibbing."

"No sir."

"How can you be so sure?" Girth asked.

"Someone in the boot of their car was waving a small swastika." I crossed my fingers behind my back.

"Oh really…" Girth shook his head in disbelief.

"My son doesn't tell tales," Mother said. "Jonathan, when you say waving, do you mean signalling?"

"Yes, Mother. Please, their life's in danger."

"You've done the right thing, Jonathan," Girth said. "I'll call Sergeant Grant. Please, Mrs Markham, can you find my gardener, while I make the call?"

When the police arrived, Reverend Girth explained what had occurred.

"Which way did they go?" Sergeant Grant asked me.

"Past the church, so I followed them by keeping close to the trees."

"Hmm, with its views out to the sea, the castle is an ideal lookout," Grant said. "Right, you stay here with your mother. Let's go."

"No. Mother and I must come with you."

"It's too dangerous."

"You need me to identify them. So my Mother must come with us."

"Come on then. Reverend, follow behind."

Mother and I climbed into the police car driven by P.C Lansky. Behind us, in the Reverend's car, was March, the gardener and Harrison, the gravedigger. The track took us directly there. The landscape was unrecognisable from the Anglo-Saxon Britain I had seen a moment ago.

Grant stuck his arm out the window and signalled to the car behind to slow down.

"Stop here, Vicar!" he shouted. "Best to travel on foot. Right lad, which way did they go?"

I froze. The open land had gone. A forest now covered the footpath Redwold must have taken to the church. A movement in the branches over my head made me glance up. Through a tangle of branches and leaves I spotted the curve of a squirrel's tail.

"Remember what happened with Jonah?" a voice from afar said.

I hesitated, not daring to look at Mother.

"Where did the car go?" Reverend asked impatiently.

"Shall I show you?"

"Yes, yes," said Grant.

"Someone passed through here. More than one Ah'd say." March pointed to some crushed plants. "They were dragging something or someone."

"Then we'll follow the trail," Grant said, ignoring me.

We entered the castle via a tumbled-down wall into what must have been the courtyard. I tried to recall the scene and the exact location of the tunnel entrance. Something hit my head; at my feet was an acorn. Another hit me and I looked up and saw Ratatosk sitting on the ruined battlement.

While the others searched in a different direction, the squirrel made his way along the wall and then dropped from view. I hurried after him.

"Jonathan where—?"

Sergeant Grant abruptly silenced Mother. "Hush, Mrs Markham."

I pushed my way through the shrubs and nearly fell down the tunnel entrance. I went to find the others.

"Give us fifteen minutes then get help," Grant told Girth, as the rest of us turned on our torches.

After leaving Mother with the Reverend, Grant led the rest of us. In the darkness, Lansky touched my shoulder, his features in his torchlight hard and bitter. "Boy, how did you find your way in the dark?"

I hesitated. As I opened my mouth to tell another lie, a piercing scream filled the tunnel. A hand covered my mouth, as Grant whispered, "Keep quiet."

We turned the corner in the corridor and froze. The sound of chattering German voices filling the space.

In a hushed tone, Grant said, "March, take Jonathan with you. Let the vicar know we'll need more help."

In the rectory Mother and I sat drinking tea, when a sound something like gunfire was heard in the distance. For a couple of hours Reverend Girth paced the floor nervously making small talk.

Just as we all started to relax the doorbell clattered to life. The sound of excited voices filled the hallway making Mother rush to the doorway. She stood frozen at the sight of a man with a deep gash over his right eye, a blood-stained face, torn clothing and his right arm in a sling.

"Oh, John!" Mother rushed into the man's arms.

"My darling Ruth," Father flinched. "Ouch, not so tight. I've a few cracked ribs, no doubt." He smiled at me. "Hello son. I've been told I'm to thank you for saving my life."

The sound of my parents' laughter floated up to me, even on such a sad day as later we'd be attending Granny's funeral. In the yard, the chickens were happily scratching around in the newly cleared garden. After the weekend

Father has to return to London for questioning by his superiors. He hopes to return soon.

I held the golden nut up to the light. In its surface there's a carving of a shadow clock. On the bed's canopy Ratatosk sat chirring at me. I placed the nut on a chest of drawers and waited. He leapt down and sniffed the nut before picking it up in his teeth. As he took the nut in his paws rigor mortis spread over his body from the tip of his tail across his body, until the light in his beady eyes went out. I picked him up and he was just a carved squirrel again.

"Jonathan!" Mother called. "It's time to go."

I placed Ratatosk on the shelf beside Granny's book. The cover now showed the children waving from the battlements of a ruined castle.

As we waited to enter the church Father said, "I hear you and your mother had quite an adventure in London. You'll find it too peaceful living here, Jonathan."

I laughed. "Reverend Girth's grandson, Thomas, said we can go out on some real adventures before school starts next term."

"Shh, it's time to say goodbye to Granny." Mother took Father's arm. "The church looks full."

To Wish Upon a Star

As the inky sky began to lighten, luminous arcs of brilliant blue and yellow flashed diagonally towards the horizon. In the distance against the retreating darkness the mountain tops shimmered with a halo of silvery gold light as day regained its place once more.

Estella, with a heavy heart after another wasted night, stepped away from the reinforced glass window. What else could she do? She knew she couldn't afford to miss the opportunity to win her heart's desire if the legend was true.

She swung the weighty protective curtain aside. It caught her delicate lace robe, pulling it off her creamy shoulders. As it fell back into place, it blocked out the growing heat of the morning light. She wondered after last night's disappointment, if the forces would be stronger tonight now the Belili Festival had begun. The festival celebrated the return of the first spring moon as it rose over the planet of Beltane. With its return came the first meteor shower of the season. Estella felt positive that she would get her wish granted this time.

The only sound that echoed around the viewing tower, in the granite castle Estella called home, was the slapping of her bare feet, as she crossed the stone-tiled floor. She shivered and pulled her robe back up onto her shoulders, tightening the belt. She wasn't really aware of the cold, as she headed for the stairs that descended into the living quarters buried deep underground.

Once she reached the corridor that led to the bedrooms, she paused briefly. Before her was a solid fireproof door. For a second her hesitation took her by surprise. Allowing her mind to relax the tension left her body and she began to key in the numbers needed to enter.

"Remember, this is all still relatively new to you," she spoke her thoughts aloud.

At the precise moment the door slid open, a picture of Hyman, her life partner flashed across her mind. She sighed gently at the image, recalling with such delight the sight of him lying asleep on his side, covered only by a finely woven silk sheet. She had lain awake listening to his soft and steady breathing, unable to sleep. What kept her from the arms of Morpheus were her thoughts.

She had discovered, within the Delta Mining Community's archive, videos containing information new to her. Now her mind seemed stuck on a loop, replaying the scenes over again. She tried to comprehend the meaning behind the groups of people known as *'families'*, but was left confused. She had managed to understand that heading the group was a male, who was known as the *father*, and a female known as the *mother*. There were other groups, also known as *family,* who comprised two of either sex, but her main interest centred on the female known as *Mother* and the mother's power to be *with child*. This knowledge created within Estella the obsession to be *with child*.

She had waited for Hyman's sleep to deepen, knowing he would release his grip on her, as he turned onto his side. Once he had she was able to ease herself out of the bed and had gone to the viewing tower to watch at the window for the first shooting star.

At first, she hadn't grasped the full meaning, not fully understanding how to unlock the secret of creation. She began to hunt through hours of video footage, witnessing the happiness the family had shared, while playing, eating and living together. She had wondered whether the men and women on the screen had created their *children* in a similar sort of way as Hyman had created their home; carving it out of living rock. There was only one reference she had found which led her to believe that the mothers created their children within themselves. This small piece of knowledge had been so amazing, it had left her with an empty craving that had created an obsession in her for a smaller version of Hyman and herself.

Once the fire door buzzed open, Estella stepped through. It softly closed behind her, as she hesitated trying to decide what to do next.

"If I tried to return to Hyman's side, my coldness will wake him. He'll ask me where I've been. No, it's much better for him to find me in the bathing room, should he wake."

She hung her robe on a hook and released the array of grips that held her blonde hair in a topknot. On entering the misting cubicle, she waited while a light scanned her body to calculate the amount of water needed. Estella's mind filled with thoughts about the shooting stars, recalling how she had come across the legend while searching the archives.

Once the misting light had finished, tiny jets of warm water began spraying her from above and all the sides of the cubicle. She turned slowly to allow the mist to dampen her body and hair, while she pondered on the finer details of the shooting star legend, wondering why it hadn't given a full explanation.

She knew the missing data would help to empower her wish, but so far she hadn't been able to clarify whether it was the first shooting star she saw, or the very first one of the season that she needed to wish upon?

All she really knew about the shooting stars was that they came twofold. At the beginning of the year, which was known as Candlemas, and then again at the year's end during the Winter Solstice. She hadn't been able to ask Hyman about the legend, which meant she needed to take a gamble. Logic had told her that the power of the wish would be greater at the beginning of the season, rather than the end.

Once the misting cubicle had completed its first cycle, a blue hue emanated from above and travelled down the full length of her body. While she waited for it to finish, her mind went back to the legend.

She couldn't understand the logic of it. According to the data she had read, at the beginning of the spring festival, if you wished upon the first bright shooting star of the season it would grant your heart's desire. However, by the end of the year, the same legend also foretold that the inhabitants of the planet needed to offer prayers to their many Gods to help them survive the long, cold winter months.

"Why only one wish?" she muttered, turning around in the blue light. "It makes me feel as though I'm putting my wants and needs above that of the whole community."

After cleansing her body of any harmful bacteria, the programme moved onto its rinsing cycle. As Estella turned in the mist, she ran her hands over her fine curves and full, soft breasts, trying to imagine what changes would happen if she were to be with child. Finally, the misting cubicle filled with warm air to dry off her body and hair.

"How wonderful it will be when we are a family," she muttered stepping out and gathering up her robe, and dropping it into a washer. With her mind still on the legend, Estella pulled on her cream linen dress and re-pinned her hair into place.

There were many questions she needed answering about creation. She knew Hyman and the other miners understood the geological structure of the planet, but what about the creation of life.

She let out a sigh and checked herself in the mirror. Her questioning eyes sparkled back at her.

"I shall just have to solve the mystery for myself," she told her reflection. "*Hyman* would just laugh at me for indulging in such primitive nonsense."

Estella had arrived on the desolate planet only six months ago. At first she had felt despondent, unable to process every new experience. However, the beauty of her new home with its clean lines and natural features ignited her curiosity. The black granite towers of castle-like buildings dotted the surface of the planet and glistened in the burning light of the planet's two suns.

Hyman, a mining engineer and designer, explained that the towers were not only where the miners lived, but they had an important job. Firstly, they were oxygen-pumping towers, which allowed the men to move freely below. Also they operated as vents that released the build-up of heat from the mines, deep within the bowels of the planet.

She clearly remembered being in awe of the tall, iron-muscular man, dressed in light brown cotton trousers and a plain white tunic. Unlike the striking surroundings he had a realistic quality about him that won her heart. She couldn't take her eyes off him loving his strong features, the soft lines around his eyes and his full lips. When he spoke the sound of his firm, but steady voice left her speechless. She drank in Hyman's excitement as he guided her around her new home. She followed in his wake. He led her from room to room, explaining as they went the idea behind having the living quarters built deep within the bedrock of the planet.

"By centralising the main living space and having all the other rooms leading off from it by a series of easy-to-operate air and fire doors, I was able to construct the viewing towers and utility rooms as separate entities from the main body of the castle. This not only allows us to keep our living quarters at a steady temperature but also so much cooler than the outside world."

Estella just listened and nodded.

"It also keeps us safe and gives us more freedom to move around without wearing cumbersome oxygen tanks and heat protective clothing," Hyman said.

She knew he was watching her reactions.

"The harsh reality of the outer landscape makes this planet one of the most difficult to inhabit." He continued with a sweeping gesture of his hand around the room. "With that in mind, I wanted each of the rooms to reflect a perfect sense of balance. By harmonizing the colour scheme of pale greens, blues, and yellows, hopefully it will give its inhabitants a sense of security, while being at one with the natural environment outside."

Estella became aware he had finished speaking. As his eyes brightened the lines around them and his lips became more defined as his smile illuminated his countenance. He reached out and caressed her cheeks. His touch created a strange warming sensation in her body and she lowered her eyes.

"Good," he'd said.

She waited for him to enlighten her to why she was good, but instead he just nodded. She wondered if he was expecting her to ask some questions, but she couldn't think of any.

Aware of some unease within the silence, she longed to hear his voice, for him to continue explaining the aspects of her new home and her role within it, but he said nothing. She waited conscious only of her thoughts. After a moment he slipped his hand into hers. His grip was strong yet gentle, even though his hands were rough to her touch. Now he guided her with his arm around her waist as they continued the tour of the house. They climbed a wide stone staircase and stopped before a curtained panoramic window. She registered the deepening tone of his voice as he emphasised the seriousness of what he was saying.

"As beautiful as the view may be, my dear, it's very important that these curtains are kept in place at all times. They are sensitive to heat and light and are here to protect us."

He pointed beyond them. Across the wide balcony three huge domed spheres rose into the night sky. Like Hyman the other wealthy miners had chosen to build their granite castles facing the domed gardens of sheer wonder forming an oasis of flowing water, plants, and trees.

"The gardens," he explained, "are not just things of beauty, but help to sustain life on this difficult, but wealthy planet. We have succeeded, where others have failed, by bringing with us wildlife that has flourished. Thus supplying us with fresh food, which the early explorers could only dream of when they came to colonise the planets within Delta-V.

As he spoke the granite mountains glistened in the clear sky and drew Estella's attention. Like dazzling jewels their brightness would have blinded anyone who didn't have a curtain or light sensitive reinforced glass to protect them. As they made their way back downstairs he continued explaining the many features of her new home.

"The lighting throughout the house is set to coincide with the changing artificial seasons outside. It also helps to keep our body clock in check, making sure we get enough sleep. The early settlers decided the best hope for survival here was to be in tune with the planet itself."

"I understand," she said, smiling at him.

"That's very good." He returned her smile, which pleased her. "I know this is all new to you, Estella. I'm sure you will soon feel at home here with me. Come let me show you the kitchen."

For the first three months she found her routine pleasurable. After sharing breakfast with her, Hyman left for work. Her chores were simple enough, making sure his clothes were ready for the next day, the house was dust free, and meals prepared ready for his homecoming. Working in a hot atmosphere the miners sweated, so they changed clothes every hour throughout their long working day, arriving home shattered, grimy, and hungry.

One evening Estella found herself becoming a little impatient with Hyman while she waited for him to shower and slip into something more comfortable, ready to dine, as he had finished work later than usual.

Everything had been ready on time. She had already set the dining table and transported their meal upstairs to the viewing tower, before he'd come home. Throughout the meal she found their conversation laboured. She had given up, unable to think of anything more to say.

By the time she began to clear the table she could no longer contain her disappointment. She understood he was tired, but she had waited patiently for his stimulating conversation, as she had nothing else to fill her long, uneventful days. Hyman laid his cutlery down and reached for his I-screen without saying a word to her.

Estella's isolation took on a physical form, as she finished her chores. She took her place beside him and watched with him as the two suns set over the mountains, marking the end of another dissatisfying day for her. Hyman sensed something in the atmosphere and lowered his I-screen, his eyes searching her face.

"What's wrong, my dear?"

Taken aback by his serious tone she said, "Is this all there is to my life? Just cleaning, cooking and sharing recipes, new cleaning ideas and small talk with the other women while you chat about more interesting things with the other miners? I find women's things inferior."

Hyman's smile broadened, as she lowered her eyes and whispered, "Is it so wrong of me to say so?"

"Not at all, my dear. I'm pleased you want to expand your mind. Come, come." He took her soft hand in his and led her downstairs.

They entered via a reinforced door she hadn't noticed before. After pressing his finger onto a pad, the door slid open. In the room large comfortable chairs faced a huge screen on one wall. Hyman tapped on a panel and a disc appeared which he placed into a slot. After a few moments a group of people appeared on the screen. An informative voice began to explain how the first men had arrived to extract the planet's vast rich deposits of minerals and precious metals.

"Everything you need to know about the history of this planet and more are in these," he said. "Now my dear," he said, "I shall programme the door so you can open it, but you must only come here while I'm at work. I expect all your other household chores to be done, too." Estella clapped her hands together in excitement as Hyman pulled her to him kissing the top of her head.

Now their mealtimes became the highlight of her day, as the conversation flowed more freely. She enjoyed his praise and laughter, as she chatted about all the new discoveries learnt from the library.

"My sweet darling, Estella," he said, kissing her lightly on the brow while brushing her hair back from her dark eyes. "What silly things you're filling your head with, but I'm glad you're enjoying learning for yourself."

"They aren't silly things." She pushed him away playfully. "Do you not ever wonder what life is like back on the Mother Planet, where the sky was once a gentler blue and everywhere was green?"

She felt Hyman tense as he rose. He crossed to the window, pushed the curtain aside and placed his hands on the glass. She wanted to stop him, as she saw the penetrating heat register on his face and the sadness within his eyes, as his reflection revealed in the glass. Estella wanted to understand how such emotions would drive someone to hurt themselves. Aware all too soon that the heat of the day would be completely gone she knew their time in the tower was nearly over, as the killing cold of the night would soon drive them below ground again.

"Earth. That's what it was called, Estella. Mother Earth," he said, tears trickling down his cheeks.

"Do you remember it?"

"No, I'm far too young. I know only the stories of its existence," he said, rubbing his hand across his face.

"It must have been a wonderful place," she said dreamily. "Can you imagine walking about outside in air you can breathe freely, while listening to birdsong and picking wild flowers?"

He turned to her. She noticed that lights across the colony were slowly going out behind him.

"Yes, I've often wondered what it must have been like to enjoy such freedom from fear, but still we have a wonderful, if restricted life here. Come, my love," he whispered, reaching for her hand. "It's time to sleep." He kissed the back of her hand and led her down to their bedroom.

She stood before him. He slipped the loosely fitted gown from her shoulders and it pooled at her feet. Then, one at a time, he removed the grips from her hair and with his fingertips he brushed it out, before kissing the top of her shoulders. Then, in one effortless sweep of his arms, he scooped her up and laid her gently down on the bed, before climbing in beside her. Estella hoped tonight would be the night when his kisses released his passion for her, but instead, he gently stroked her cheek, told her how beautiful she was, before hugging her to him, as sleep overpowered him.

Her mind began to recite the words of love and romance she'd discovered while reading the reference books. Was it possible, she wondered, if she shared those words of love with him, that somehow it might unlock his passion for her and trigger the creation of the child she longed for?

Her mind raced with a question that had been bothering her. If it was only natural for men and women living together to create children, then why weren't there any in the mining community? She had wanted to ask Hyman, but after his comment about her thoughts being *silly things*, she was reluctant to do so.

At the monthly meeting with the other miners, she had questioned the women, but like her, they knew nothing about children. When she tried to explain what she understood about them, the women just laughed at her.

"Children indeed. We have enough to do with cooking, cleaning and seeing to our men's needs to worry about such things."

Last night's failure made her more determined, as she lay in the darkness waiting for Hyman to slip into a deeper sleep. She placed her hand on her flat stomach and chanted her longing into the darkness.

Tomorrow marked the beginning of the Belili Festival, when the Goddess of Trees, Love and the Underworld returned. Estella hoped it would mark the beginning of a new life for her and hopefully for the child she longed for too. She was excited at the thought of passing on her new knowledge to her children and to the other women.

The moment she had waited for all day arrived. Hyman's

breathing altered and he rolled away from her. She checked the clock and found that there was just another hour to go.

Her thoughts shifted to when she'd found the entry in an I-screen about the mythology of shooting stars and wishes. The revelation had at last given her the missing information she had sought.

As Hyman's breathing slowed to a steady pace, Estella briefly wondered whether the other women were right. Why couldn't she be as contented as they were? After all they had only been on the planet for the same amount of time as she had. Yet something within her had triggered this growing need.

Her normal routine allowed her to slip out of bed long before Hyman woke, but still she was always cautious not to disturb him. She stepped away from the bed and unconsciously turned to admire her life's partner. Hyman lay on his side. Beneath the sheet, highlighted by the growing shimmering light in the room, the fine details of his muscular body stood out clearly for her to enjoy.

She studied his face. Below his eyelids she saw rapid eye movement and wondered if he dreamt about the same things as she did – to have a child in their image? Automatically she reached out and brushed the strands of his brown hair away from his shoulders. His face, handsome with full lips and high-bridged nose, that gave it an air of dignity, was as familiar to her as her own face, she thought, catching a shadowy glimpse of herself in the mirror over the bed. Estella recalled their first encounter six months ago, glad he had chosen her to share his life's journey. Hyman was highly respected in their community she had learned. He was a kind, thoughtful man, so why didn't he display the passion that the poetry and novels from the old world talked about within their pages?

As the lights began to flicker she knew the time for star-wishing had arrived and headed for the door. Just as she reached for the door panel Hyman rolled onto to his back. She froze, fearing he would wake.

If he woke now, her opportunity would be gone. She knew he would question her sanity. After all a man of science wouldn't hold with such utter rubbish, even she had questioned the science behind making wishes on falling pieces of long dead planets, but she had no other choice. As the door closed Estella hurried up the stairs to the viewing tower.

She stepped out onto the balcony. The air buzzed with electricity and tingled against her skin. She had wanted to know more. Would her wish be more potent if made inside the tower, or outside? She ignored the dryness in her nostrils and throat as she lifted her arms to the heavens. Estella focused on how pure the stars looked against the inky sky high above her. She took a few tentative steps forward. Her fine lace gown lifted from her body as a surprisingly warm light breeze raced across her skin like a lover's touch. She let out a soft moan of pleasure as the first shower of fast moving meteors lit up the night sky with brilliant flashes.

As her mind acknowledged the good fortune such a magnificent display of shooting stars would bring the colony, a pounding noise broke the silence. At first she thought it was in her head. Estella glanced over her shoulder. Hyman was banging on the reinforced glass. She registered that he was gesturing to her, but his words were lost. Powerful warmth raced up her naked body and through her flowing hair. As her eyes closed against the brightness of the glowing embers, she felt nothing more.

Hyman rested his forehead against the hot glass and let his arm drop. He stepped away from the window, allowing the heavy protective curtain to fall back into place, blocking out the view. The cosmic storm snatched away the pile of glittering ash on the other side of the glass.

Hyman shook his head, letting out a long sigh. "Not again. Why on earth do they keep doing that to themselves?"

As the swirling dust carried away the fading image of Estella's beauty, Hyman wondered for the third time what it was he was doing wrong. He took no pleasure in watching all his hard work going to waste.

"Perhaps I'm being a little overzealous with the programming in making my Life Partner Android too realistic, by adding all those extras, like free thought and retained information?"

On his way down to his laboratory he began to question his desire to have a precise copy of his beautiful wife, Estella, to comfort him through their long separations.

"Oh well, at least it'll keep me busy for the next six months. By the time the meteor storm has finished I might have completed another replacement. I wonder how the other guys are coping with their L.P.As," Hyman muttered, as the door closed behind him.

Shelved

"I do so hate it when people don't respect books," the librarian said, narrowing his eyes as he peered over his spectacles.

I nodded in agreement. We stood in his office. I wanted only to pay my fine and be gone.

He continued, without pausing. "They treat them as if they're their own, bending corners and scribbling notes in the margins. Then there are the tea stains and the devil-only-knows-stains. Can you believe it?"

I nodded like a donkey, wishing he would cut to the chase. I had tried to interrupt him on numerous occasions, when I had been late bringing back books before, so I knew it wasn't wise to do so when he was on a roll.

He carried on. "I've even known people to bring them back with the pages all crinkled and stuck together, after they had dropped them in the bath." The librarian's eyes became black slits. He lowered his nasally voice and said, "What sort of respect does that show for books?"

I shrugged, shook my head and glanced surreptitiously at my watch. I was running late and wasn't about to engage in a long conversation about the state of the library's books. If my wife had just returned mine, as I had asked her to on numerous occasions over the past few weeks, I wouldn't be stuck here listening to Mr Jobsworth. Even though I felt he had a valid point.

He leant forward and spoke as if to a five year old. "These... books... are... not... yours, only yours to borrow."

I stepped back. His breath seemed to scorch my face. He leant in closer, invading my personal space. A stale odour from his breath filled my nostrils, as his eyes bored into mine.

"This is a fact many people seem to forget. How would it be if I were to take something of yours? Something that's precious to you, Mr Logan."

Unable to stop myself, I coughed. "I'm sorry," I spluttered, "how much is the fine this time?"

"A fine? That's it, just a fine?" his voice rose as he closed the gap between us. "You think if you hand over some money it'll all be forgotten!" He turned his back on me and shrugged his shoulders.

I glanced about the room, aware of it for the first time. He had called it his office, but it wasn't one of those modern open-planned, state-of -the -art numbers, but a small, windowless room.

Apart from the librarian and me, the room contained a large wooden desk, a chair, and an unusual number of leather-bound books in all sizes and colours instead of the normal well-thumbed paperbacks and the standard hardbacks you normally associate with a library. These filled the shelves and spilled over into piles which covered the desk and floor. I took a deep breath, pulled at my tie, trying to loosen it, while glancing at my watch annoyed to find I had missed the first important meeting of the day. I sighed at the stupidity of it all. If I could just pay what I owed, I could've been on my way.

An overwhelming sensation, as if the walls were closing in, made me panic. I let my breath out slowly, trying to remain calm. As I caught my breath a familiar, comforting smell of musty, old books filled my nostrils. I tried to relax and took another deeper breath and started coughing.

Something nauseous and penetrating lurked beneath the books' odour. Strangely recognizable, though I couldn't quite name it. Involuntarily I caught my breath, as a thought tumbled through my head. The smell was a strange mixture of damp bonfires and wet ash, which seemed quite outlandish.

I studied the librarian's back. He seemed ill at ease with himself. His gangly frame was clearly visible through his ill-fitting jacket. As he faced me again, his jet-black, piggy eyes narrowed and lanced into mine. He sucked in air through his nostrils. With a hiss, his face became sharper, almost angular, as he continued his berating.

"You people make me sick. Money. You think that's the answer to everything. You pay up and go. Well, surprise, surprise, Mr Logan, not this time."

"Hey! Hang on a minute. They're just damn books and not good ones at that."

He smiled sardonically, pointing a long, bony finger at me. "What? You think that makes a difference, whether you enjoyed them or not? You just don't get it, do you?" He gestured to my motley collection of library books, "Someone else missed enjoying these books, while you took your time returning them."

"You can't speak to me like that. I want to see the manager!" My voice echoed back at me from around the room.

"You want what?" His voice, low and mocking, seemed to grow in size. "Do you really think I'm interested in what you want? Tell me, Mr Logan, have you ever given a thought to the needs of others? To you they're just books, but you don't have to deal with customers' dissatisfaction every day. They come in here, demanding this or that book," he scoffed. "They come with expectations hoping to find just the book they want after all it's a library."

"Well, I'm sorry. I didn't know." I tried to sound sympathetic, recalling reading somewhere about how to cope in a hostage situation. The first golden rule is to get the kidnapper to relate to you as a fellow human being; to win them over. I smiled and softened my tone, "Don't get me wrong. I do understand. It must be hard to keep everyone happy."

"You've no idea!" he pointed that accusing finger

again. "Books are my life." He gestured to the ones surrounding us. "Within these books are stories of the great and humble, of ordinary people who led extraordinary lives, from politicians through to criminals and finally those of *everyday little lives.*"

He picked up a small, red book from a pile in front of him. He held it to his chest, stroked the cover and while running his forefinger up and down the spine. It seemed almost obscene. He looked straight through me. "Are you one of those people who 'Google' everything?"

I lied. "Me? No, I love to look things up in books. I've got quite a collection at home."

His eyes enlarged.

"No, no you misunderstand me. They are mine. I bought them, or my friends gave them to me as presents. You know the sort of thing, coffee table books, everyone has, but no one reads." I laughed nervously, but could see I was losing him. I grinned insanely.

"I hate the internet. I hate it when I hear people say books are out-dated." He slammed his fist down on the desk making the piles of books and me jump.

"Oh, I quite agree," I muttered.

"You agree?" His voice rose to the next level as his eyes widened. "You agree books... are history!"

"No, no, with you. I meant I agree with you. There's nothing like holding a book, turning real pages and then there's the smell of them... wonderful!"

"I'm glad you think so—" His lips curled into a disgusting unnatural smile as he gestured to the chair. "Now, Mr Logan, please do sit down."

I stood my ground. "No, I feel far more comfortable standing, if you don't mind. Look, I'm a tad busy. You've made your point. I'm extremely sorry about bringing the books back late. It won't happen again, I promise. I'll—"

He stepped towards me and through gritted teeth, in a low menacing voice, said, "I do mind, Mr Logan. Now sit!"

I sat. My mind reeled, knowing I wasn't going to make it to my second meeting. The one I had especially prepared for. The one where I told my boss exactly what he could do with his stupid job, but now this insignificant Jobsworth was stopping me from having that pleasure. Was I never going to leave the room? I ran my finger around my collar again, and tried to calm myself. "Look Mr Err Mmm." I looked for his name badge, but couldn't find one. I tried to recall whether he had been wearing one when he stopped me at the door of the library. Come to think of it, I'm pretty sure he wasn't the normal librarian I dealt with. Hindsight is such a marvellous thing.

"My name's Wormwood. Mr Natas Wormwood," he said.

"Oh, well, Mr Wormwood. I think you're overreacting. I'm pleased to meet someone dedicated to their work. And obviously, you feel deeply about the books, but as a tax payer, I do feel I have some say in—"

I stood up proud that I was keeping a level head and civil tongue. I continued, making a valid point about how my taxes paid for his wages, when he interrupted me.

"I'm so glad you sympathize with me, Mr Logan, not many do. So you'll fully understand why I cannot just let this go. One must always pay one's debts in full, just like one's taxes." He smiled menacingly, with narrowed lips, as he leant forward.

I smelt sulphuric acid on his stale breath. It lingered in my nostrils and on my tongue. I swallowed hard.

He stretched out his hand placing his index finger on the centre of my forehead. My skin crawled from his repulsive touch, as though his fingertip was penetrating my very being. I furiously gulped in air. "Hey, what are you

114

doing?" My legs gave beneath me. I sat down with a stomach retching thud.

"I'm taking what's mine to take, Mr Logan."

I tried to focus on the room, but the stabbing pain in my head became so intense that I was unable to keep my eyes open and closed them in an effort to shut out the pain.

I sensed Mr Wormwood had moved away from me. I opened my eyes and tried to lever myself off the chair, but my legs no longer seemed to belong to me. I looked down at my hands and saw they were changing too.

My fingers began to flatten out and expand. At the same time odd words began to appear on them, followed by whole sentences. I was fascinated. The words had been spoken by me, while I argued with my wife, this morning, over the library books. I inhaled deeply in an effort to remain calm. Not quite believing what was happening. The smell that earlier on I hadn't recognised became stronger and filled the room. Ink! That's what it was, ink! But why ink?

My body began to vibrate, as the room filled with the sounds of whirls and clunks that added to my confusion. My hands had reformed into one flat sheet as my arms joined them too. And still the words kept coming. Some familiar, half remembered and spoken in haste. Plenty had been spoken cruelly, while some were said with regret, but now unable to be taken back.

I slumped in the chair, with no fight left. I focused on the sound, recognising its significance.

A printer? What printer? I didn't remember seeing one when we entered. Mr Wormwood stood on the far side of his desk, with a lopsided smile plastered on his face. I studied him. His skin had taken on a leathery-tanned look. It suddenly occurred to me that he seemed oddly familiar. He winked as if in acknowledgement of my recognition. I felt a raw clinging chill wash through me for not understanding

115

that sooner. Though he isn't someone you would expect to find in a library.

Under the circumstances it seemed such an odd kind of thought to be having, as I felt myself fading away. I watched spellbound, as the room filled with strange text in streams of familiar dialogue and sentences of conversations I'd had with my boss recently, as well as arguments with my mother-in-law and not to mention my underhandedness against some of my colleagues.

When Mr Wormwood spoke again, it seemed to come from afar. "Mr Logan, you were given every chance to pay such a small debt. I gave you many warnings about returning your books on time. You might make fine speeches, but in the end it's all down to you." He smiled that unnatural smile of his again.

The room began to grow much bigger, as I felt myself falling through the air. Then to my utter amazement I saw him pick up something small from the chair, where moments before I'd been sitting. He hugged it to his bony chest. It was a little brown book with my name embossed, in gold lettering, on its spine.

As a dark shadow enveloped him, he fondled the book, caressing it, "Such an uninteresting life, you've had, Mr Logan, but still it's worth adding to my collection of... *unworthy souls.*"

From somewhere and nowhere I watched Natas Wormwood toss me on the top of a tottering pile of books that stood in a dusty corner. He rubbed his bony hands together in delight and turned dancing out of the room. That's when I was sure I caught a glimpse of his tail.

So take heed, my dear readers, never cross a librarian and make sure you always take your books back on time, or else you might just find yourself shelved like the rest of us in this everlasting Library of the Dead.

Perfect Justice

I used to love my job, but not anymore. For fifteen years I enjoyed working for the building company Davidson Ltd. The wages were better than most. Then one morning everything changed. I don't like to use the word *hate* to describe how I felt on waking, but dread wasn't a strong enough word. Just the thought of having to deal with a certain person set my pulse racing.

Three years ago I always liked to arrive early for work to ensure everything was ready for Mr Davidson's arrival. *Efficiency* was his keyword. I always checked the emails for any new orders and restocked anything needed to complete jobs on time. Any problems or late orders I would print a copy of the details and place them on Mr Davidson's desk, along with a fresh cup of tea, so he had plenty of warning if anything might cause a delay.

"Timing is everything," Mr Davidson would say. "The earlier we know about problems, the quicker we can resolve it. Get your timing right and you can beat your competitors easily, while saving time and money, Brenda."

Then everything changed. I arrived at my usual time, after stopping off at a local newsagent to pick up a pint of milk, along with some fresh cakes for Mr Davidson's elevenses. The kettle had only just boiled, when to my surprise my boss buzzed. I hastily checked my watch. He was in early too. I made his tea and hurried through.

"Ah Brenda," he beamed.

I returned his smile. Anxious for the first time in all the years I had worked for him. I was about to ask if there were any problems, when he saved me the bother.

"Thank you for my tea. Please set it down there," he said, clearing a spot on his desk. "I have some good news."

I raised my notebook ready to start a dictation.

"No, no," he said. "The news doesn't really affect the rest of the staff. Today someone new is starting and I want you to show them the ropes. Please get them settled in as soon as possible, Brenda."

"Oh, yes, of course, Mr Davidson."

"Good." He reached for his phone and I took it as a sign of dismissal.

I lingered, unsure quite what he meant by *showing the ropes* to this unnamed person. When he showed no sign of acknowledging me, I gave a light cough.

"Yes, Brenda?" He held the phone from his ear; his finger paused over a button.

"Mr Davidson, hmm… what time will the person be arriving and what department am I to show them around?"

"Department? No, no, Brenda. She'll be working with you."

"Me!" I couldn't keep the shock out of my voice. Aghast that Mr Davidson felt the need to have someone else working with me.

I arrived back early from lunch and was shocked to discover a new desk in my office. It was much smaller than mine and it stood in a small dark alcove, facing a large free standing unit full of old company files.

I set my handbag down on my desk, as panic raced through my gut. *Where in hell was my computer?* Standing in its place was a new one. For a second I couldn't breathe and leant on the desk. All my work was gone, along with my belongings too. I let my breath out slowly. Shocked I reached for the phone and stabbed at the buttons.

"Aha, Brenda, you're back at last," Mr Davidson said.

Back at last! I hung the phone up. What in hell did he mean? My lunch break had not finished. Unfazed by my look of annoyance he turned to speak to someone just out of my view. As my boss stepped aside a petite, bleached-blonde woman hesitated in the doorway. She smiled meekly up at him. Mr Davidson rested his hand on her back in a reassuring way. The woman didn't look like the type to need reassurance, not with her pencilled-in eyebrows and long red painted nails. Her attire of tight fitted white jeans, a skinny ribbed red jumper, and black stiletto heeled boots was more suited for an evening in a nightclub rather than for work.

"Brenda, this is Sabrina Perfect," my boss said, smiling broadly.

Ms Perfect lowered her head and smiled coquettishly at me, but my radar picked up trouble.

"She's here to help you." Mr Davidson pointed to the desk in the alcove. "Please move your belongings to that desk there."

To my surprise I realised that the tatty collection of dictionaries, *English Grammar,* and *Idiot's Guide To Computers* and spread sheet books were mine, so was the computer. Relief washed over me. I grinned through gritted teeth. "No need, sir. Someone has already done it."

"That's great. So, no time wasted, you can both get on with the job," he said to me, before turning to Sabrina. "Now, I hope you'll settle in quite quickly, Sabrina. If you need to know anything, please don't hesitate to ask Brenda."

Ms Perfect gave him a bright smile and then to my horror she winked at Mr Davidson, as he left the room.

From then on my serenity was shattered. No longer a shy little Miss, Sabrina became a chatterbox. Unsurprisingly her pet subject was herself. As for showing her the ropes I had to teach her the basics. She knew nothing, not even how to turn a computer on. Why did Mr Davidson feel I needed her here to run the office? Hadn't I been more than efficient?

By the end of the first day, all I really wanted to do was

to show her how to hang herself. After the first week I was shattered and mentally drained. Once I used to be able to work at a leisurely pace. Now I seemed to spend most of my time playing catch-up with orders, while double-checking her work.

It wasn't just playing catch-up that took its toll on me, but having to endure her spiteful remarks.

"Brenda, when do you retire?"

"Retire? I'm not ready to retire yet."

"But you're old."

"Age is just a number."

"Well, when I get as old as you, I want to be doing something other than just this boring job."

I peered in her direction. She was watching again, waiting for a reaction to her comment. Whenever I caught her in the act, she wasn't a bit embarrassed and just smiled at me. My only relief came during lunchtime, or on overtime. Previously overtime wasn't something I had had to do, but it became a necessity much to my annoyance. One lunch break after Mr Davidson and Sabrina had left I settled down to work on a personal project. A knock at the door startled me. I hastily changed the screen and called, "Come in. It's unlocked,"

To my surprise Mrs Davidson entered. Tall and elegant she wore a figure-hugging dark brown tweed skirt suit and kitten-heeled black patent leather shoes that complemented not only her age, but her height and build. Her shoulder length light brown hair framed her perfectly made-up face. At first she looked quite youthful, but lines of concern around her eyes suggested to me that she was in her late forties, rather than her late thirties.

"Hello Brenda... Is my husband about?" she asked. I met her anxious face with a smile. "I'm sorry, but he's gone to lunch. Can I help?"

She hesitated for a second, before closing the door and gesturing to a chair, "May I?"

"Of course, Mrs Davidson, please do."

With poise she sat and crossed her fine ankles.

"I hope I'm not disturbing you, Brenda," she said, while glancing back at the door. "I was... hmm... well... you've worked with my husband for many years. I was wondering if..." She paused and bit her bottom lip as a heavy furrow marked her brow.

I smiled, hoping a look of patience showed on my face. That's when it dawned on me – she hadn't expected to find Mr Davidson here. She wanted to speak to me. Over the years I've worked for her husband I hadn't really had much contact with Mrs D. apart from an occasional brief phone call, "Hello, may I speak to my husband?" or in passing at the firm's Christmas do, "Happy Christmas, Brenda." Therefore, I knew this was more than just a social chitchat.

She leant forward in a conspiratorial sort of way. "What I'm trying to say, Brenda, is you know my husband almost as well as I do. So I was wondering if you've seen any changes in his behaviour just lately."

"Changes, Mrs Davidson? I'm sorry I'm not sure what you mean?"

She glanced down, tugging at her wedding ring. "Brenda, how can I put this?" She didn't meet my eyes as she spoke slowly. "What I mean is, if it's possible, could you tell me if my husband and...?" A tiny sob broke free, as she lifted her tearful eyes to meet my puzzled expression.

The proverbial penny dropped. I realised just what her fear was. I nearly laughed in the poor woman's face. "Oh, Mrs Davidson, I can assure you that your husband isn't..." I stuttered unable to complete the sentence. Personally I couldn't see Mr Davidson showing an interest in someone as shallow as Sabrina.

"Brenda, please call me Zara." A light flush coloured her cheeks as she handed me a small white business card. "All I'm asking is for you to let me know if he behaves out of character, that's all."

"I'm sorry Mrs Davidson... Zara, but..." I sought inspiration, not wanting to tell her I couldn't snoop on my boss. I studied her card for a moment and then dropped it on the corner of my desk. "Please, don't be offended, but I'm not sure if I'm the right person to ask. After all I only work for Mr Davidson."

She nodded, but I saw she wasn't satisfied.

Mrs D. studied her nails for a moment. Unlike Sabrina's long red ones, hers were short, squared, but well-manicured; a sign that she enjoyed gardening or doing housework.

"Brenda, I'm just a little concerned about my husband."

I stared at my computer wanting to get on with what I was doing before she'd interrupted. "Oh. Maybe he's anxious about the business, or something I'm not aware of?" I said.

Her face tightened and then with a half-smile, she said, "You're in a better position than I am to know about such things. Look, can I be honest with you?"

I nodded.

"This new secretary of his... she's so young."

Ahh, so little Miss Perfect was at the heart of all of this. "Well, I wouldn't call twenty-five young."

She gave a curt nod. "Why does he need her? When he's always been happy with your work, Brenda?"

I smiled. "I'm guessing with the increase in the workload, Mr Davidson has planned ahead." I said, feeling I owed some sort of loyalty to him. "That's why I'm working through my lunch break."

"Oh," she said, looking towards Sabrina's empty desk. "So why isn't she here too?"

122

My annoyance began to bubble up. I wanted to be honest, but instead I fudged the truth. "Well, she's not quite up to speed on some of the more important elements of the business. Zara, I'm sure you've nothing to worry about with Mr Davidson."

"Does *she* work *in* his office?"

"No," I said. "He buzzes me, if he wants something."

"Where are they both now?"

"Out to lunch," I said, pushing my spectacles up my nose, wishing only to get on with what I was doing.

"Together?"

"Zara, in all honesty, I cannot answer that, but I would say no. Sabrina left here alone. As you know Mr Davidson has his own private entrance into his office. I don't always know what time he leaves for lunch. Sometimes he'll call through to let me know if he's going onto another site straight afterwards. Today he didn't, so I'm sure he'll be back here by one, if you would like to wait in his office."

"No, no, that's quite all right," she said, heading for the door. "I'll see him at home." She paused briefly in the doorway. "Brenda, please contact me if you think there's something I should know about."

"Of course, Zara, I will."

Once she left, I briefly studied her business card again. The details were inscribed in gold calligraphy. I tore it up, dropping it in the waste basket and returned to my editing.

By the time Sabrina swanned in, lunchtime was well and truly over, but her lateness didn't bother me. I felt too smug to care.

"Good afternoon, Sabrina," I clicked send on an email to myself. She leant against the shelving next to my desk, looking smug too.

I smiled at her, but she remained tight-lipped.

"Is everything all right, Sabrina?"

123

She looked me up and down. "You could do so much more with yourself, Brenda. You dress like an old biddy. What's this thing you have with cardigans, woollen skirts and granny shoes? Those round metal-rimmed glasses of yours are so passé.

"Passé?" I gave a light laugh. Shocked she knew the meaning of such a word.

"Sabrina, some of us are happy with the way we are." I opened a fresh document on my screen and hoped by ignoring her; she would go back to her own desk.

Out of the corner of my eye, I saw her staring at the floor. Then she bent, picked something up and studied it briefly, before continuing, "Maybe if you focused more on your appearance, you'd have better luck in finding a bloke."

"A bloke?" I let my breath out slowly to control my temper.

"Yes, every woman needs a bloke in their life. My mum says that's what makes a woman feel completely happy."

"Every woman!" I snapped, not wishing to hear any more of her mother's wisdom.

"Yes. Nothing's going to stand in my way to be with my fellow," she stated, in a dark tone.

"I'm sure your mother is a wise lady, but you needn't concern yourself about me. Now we must concentrate on our work, so things get done a bit quicker around here."

Her bright red lips grinned back at me. She lowered her eyes, as though she was about to say something more, but I was focusing on my screen. Out of the corner of my eye, I saw her snatch something from the floor before returning to her desk.

For a while the office fell silent. I concentrated on checking the details for the company's next big project. When I say we worked in silence, I meant apart from the incessant clicking of Sabrina's plastic nails against her keyboard. I wanted so much to rip them off her fingers with pliers.

When I looked up again I was relieved to find it was nearly the afternoon tea break. I bent to pick my bag off the floor when a flash of white caught my attention. It was part of Mrs Davidson's business card. I popped it into the waste bin. I sensed Sabrina's eyes on me and knew she had more to say.

"Brenda, you're so last week's news. No decent guy would be interested in you."

"And you're not?" I knew as soon as the words were out of mouth I shouldn't have reacted.

Sabrina giggled. "My Mum said she knew the moment I was born that I was special. Perfect, in name and nature, is what she told everyone. She said that one day my face will grace the cover of every magazine and newspaper across the country, maybe even the world."

A pain crept up to my temple, as I clenched my teeth at her mother's wisdom.

She went on. "So Brenda what exactly have you got going for you? I mean unmarried at your age. Men must find you so dull and boring."

That was my fatal mistake I allowed her to goad me into telling her my most passionate secret. I poured my heart out. Like the bittersweet taste of syrup the truth dawned on me. I should've known better. The glint in her eyes wasn't admiration, or even fascination, but her acknowledgement of finding my weak spot. Now she had ammunition to use against me. That's when I started planning my first crime novel, *Death of Little Miss Perfect*.

Over the next few months I planned how to commit the perfect murder. Every free second during the day I added notes to a file I kept on my computer. Then just before home time I would email a copy to myself. In the evening, I worked on the chapters, editing as I went along.

Sabrina became my muse. Every emotion of hatred that surfaced in me during the day, I poured into my creativity, allowing the words to flow from me. One day, while there was a lull in my work, I became so engrossed in adding ideas to my file I didn't notice Sabrina come up behind me, until her reflection appeared on my screen. Luckily, I flicked onto another screen, before she could read it.

"You know, you aren't supposed to do your own writing in work's time," she said in her mocking little girl tone.

I glared at her. "Haven't you got any work to do?"

"Plenty. Unlike you, it seems."

I opened the company emails hoping she would stop harassing me, but she was nowhere near finished.

"Isn't it about time you took a reality check, Brenda? You aren't ever going to be famous. You're such a loser." She adjusted her brightly coloured butterfly hair-clips before snatching up a folder. At the door, she flicked her bleached blonde hair over her shoulders, and grinned at me as she left the office.

The next morning before I had chance to boil the kettle, my boss summoned me to his office.

"Brenda, please come through right now…" he drew out the last word.

"I've just switched on the kettle, Mr Davidson."

"Forget about my tea."

"But I—" The phone went dead in my hand and cut off my sentence.

As I entered his office he gestured impatiently to me from behind his desk without looking up. "Shut the door, Brenda. Sit down."

My stomach sunk. It wasn't like him to ask me to sit.

126

Without even making eye contact with me he went straight into what he had to say.

"It's been brought to my attention that on several occasions you've not been concentrating on your work."

I went to protest, but he silenced me with a flick of his hand.

"Up until now we've always been satisfied with your work, but just lately some important papers have gone astray."

"What papers? What are you saying?"

He glared at me. "I've been told that you're working on some book, Miss Wild—"

"But Mr Davidson it's only in my own time and break times."

"Well, I need you to concentrate more on the work you're paid for, not some future little dream of yours. Now, I'm sure you've plenty to do. And, if it's brought to my attention again, I shall have to take matters further."

I sat at my desk, fuming and re-evaluated my life. Mr Davidson had never criticised me before. I've always felt we had a great working relationship. We never engaged in personal chitchat, but there was a mutual understanding of each other. Hurt by his sudden change of attitude towards me, I began to think about all the new possibilities that could soon be opening up for me. I decided that anything was better than being stuck in an office staring at a shelf full of faded yellow files listening to Sabrina.

I clicked send on an email and muttered aloud, "Timing is everything."

The door burst open and Sabrina floated in, late as usual, humming to herself. She dumped her bag on her desk.

"Oh, good morning Brenda." Her self-satisfied smile dropped from her red lips at the sight of me. She perched on the edge of my old desk showing no sign of starting work. She briefly stared at her nails and began to chip away at the red varnish.

I wondered if Sabrina thought that I should dress in her style, with a peek-a-boo knickers skirt and ankle-breaking boots that screamed, "*Look at me! Look at me! Don't you think I'm sexy?*"

"*Timing*," I muttered, focusing on my work while praying for the strength not to strangle her.

"Brenda?"

I pressed my lips into a pinched smile. "Yes?"

"I'm sorry, but yesterday when Mr Davidson asked me if I knew where some important documents were, I told him I didn't know."

Sabrina didn't seem to notice the anger settle on my face.

"Well, how was I to know that some silly designs for a house were that important?"

"Sabrina, all files are important. Please don't tell me they were the ones with the designer's notes about building changes on them?"

"I didn't think it mattered. I knew you would be able to produce another copy after I spilt my drink on them." She sighed gave a shrug and grinned at me as chips of red varnish fluttered to the floor like blood droplets.

Dear God, I thought, *please let me put her down now.*

She waffled on, while I tried to concentrate on what she was saying, but a beautiful image of her floated into my mind. She knelt before me, begging for my forgiveness, but I was enjoying the moment too much, as I fed her fingers into the paper shredder. Suddenly the delightful vision faded as her words penetrated.

"Of course, I wouldn't let myself go like some women," she giggled girlishly. "My mum says if you want to keep your man happy you need to look after your figure, especially when you reach a certain age, Brenda."

When I didn't answer her she sat down and began to work. The image in my head reformed itself. Sabrina seated in an electric chair, wearing a metal cap and shaking as I threw the switch. I imagined her brain frying. If she had one.

Once she focused on her work, I flicked back to my original screen and carried on editing my *Disposal of the Body* chapter.

"Brenda," she drew my name out in her childish annoying voice. "Have you ever thought about Botox?

"No, I haven't."

"If I was you, I would. You could lose those frown lines."

"Is that what you use then?" I kept my eyes on my screen.

"Please... tell me you're joking? I'm far too young to use Botox, but you aren't. You could get rid of those wrinkles and—"

I was no longer listening. That's it! Rat poison. Yes, of course. Why hadn't I thought of it? I looked up to find Sabrina watching me. I smiled while trying to picture her with a gag in her mouth buried alive somewhere.

As my novel came to its completion so Sabrina's life changed forever. In her normal cryptic way she chatted to me about it, but for some reason I was unable to blank her out as I had learnt to do in the past. She smugly informed me that her mother had been right.

"Sorry, your mother was right about what?" I met her stare.

"I knew you weren't listening to me," she said in her monotone voice. "I was saying you can get away with anything if you have a winning smile."

"And you do." I said without realising that for once it sounded like I was agreeing with her.

"Thank you, Brenda. Anyway, that's how I won my Mr Right. He told me it was the first thing he noticed about me. I'm so lucky to have been born with perfect teeth." She beamed at me with a smile that had as much appeal as a mouse from a cat.

I glanced over the top of my spectacles, but in my mind all I could picture was Sabrina's corpse, laid out in a coffin, with that same painted-on smile. With a nod, I said, "It's delightful."

The morning started as it usually did with Sabrina arriving late. However, on this particular Monday morning, while the kettle was boiling, I checked my private email account and discovered an email from a publisher.

"Timing is everything." I left Mr Davidson's tea to stew, not caring about it for once. I printed off the email and began the process of deleting all my personal files from the company computer.

"Morning Brenda." Sabrina finally arrived and plonked herself down on the corner of her desk. "Has Martin spoken to you yet?"

"Don't you mean Mr Davidson?" I watched the final folder deleting and then emptied the recycle bin and history folder, before meeting her eyes.

She cocked her head on one side and smirked at me just as Mr Davidson opened his office door and called, "Brenda, please come here for a moment. Don't worry about my drink."

I slipped the email into my cardigan pocket as I entered his office.

"Please sit down." He gestured to a chair, as he perched on the front of his desk.

I noticed he looked different. Gone was his dark business

suit and formal tie. Now he wore a casual jacket and trousers. Over the weekend his hair had changed colour too. His temples no longer showed signs of grey.

"I'm sorry to have to inform you, but the company needs to make some cutbacks, and with a heavy heart Brenda—"

Before he had chance to finish his speech, I stood and smiled at him. Without another word, he handed me a letter.

"Please don't worry about working up to the end of the month. You'll find a bit extra in your pay-packet. Once you've cleared your desk, you can go."

For a moment I pondered about telling him my news, but he had already returned to his seat. As he sat staring at his computer screen I knew it was pointless to expect him to thank me for my loyalty and hard work.

On closing the office door for the last time, I grasped the email in my pocket and grinned to myself.

At my desk I found Sabrina busy packing my things into a box. She looked up with a creamy cat-like smirk.

"Dear Brenda, now, don't you go upsetting yourself." She emptied the contents of my drawer into the box. "There's no point in crying over spilt milk, as my mum is fond of saying. Though, in all honesty, you did bring it upon yourself."

"I did what?"

"You told Martin's wife about us."

"I've no idea what you're talking about, Sabrina."

"Oh yes, you did. I found part of her business card by your desk. You should have kept your nose out of other people's business. My Mum says—"

I ignored her, picked up my bag and headed for the door.

"What about your things?" she snapped.

"You keep them, you'll need them..." I allowed the door to slam shut.

So many unbelievable things have happened in the time since I've left the company. With the first print run of my book I've been busy promoting and doing signings around the country, so I hadn't really noticed how much time had passed.

In my excitement at seeing my name on the cover of my novel, I sent a signed copy to my old boss as a thank you for introducing me to Sabrina. Bitchy, I know, but hey, he did me a favour, didn't he?

While working on my second novel I rented a holiday cottage in Cornwall, a sort of self-imprisonment. One morning I decided to take a well-earned break from the writing and headed to the local shop for supplies. As I passed the newsagent window I saw Sabrina's smiling countenance staring back at me.

On entering the shop I found most of the newspapers carried the same beaming photograph of her on all their covers. However, what intrigued me most was one of the headlines, *Best-selling Novel Leads to Cold Blooded Murder*.

I purchased a copy and sat on the seawall to read it. The paper stated:

Yesterday a police spokesperson confirmed that the body of a woman found in the Sussex holiday home of the businessman, Martin Davidson, was that of his missing secretary, Miss Sabrina Perfect.

Perfect's family had reported her missing two months earlier after she failed to return home from a holiday she had taken abroad.

The paper went on to report that the police had arrested and charged Zara, the wife of Martin Davidson for the unlawful killing of Miss Perfect.

Another bizarre twist to the case has since come to light that might explain what led up to the death of Ms Perfect. A novel found at the crime scene, titled *The Perfect Murder* had been written by the former secretary of Martin Davidson, Miss Brenda Wild.

When the story broke our reporter was unable to track down the author for her reaction, but her publisher has stated that her book is now on its fourth reprint.

I lowered the newspaper, and stared out across the harbour. The gulls sailed on the light breeze. I mulled over whether sending Zara a copy of my book was a bad idea, as she may have misinterpreted my reason for sending it. Did she think it was a sign to tell her that her husband was up to no good with his new secretary?

I tucked the newspaper under my arm and headed back to the cottage knowing my publisher would be very interested in my second novel. I laughed to myself which startled a fisherman on the harbour. At least Sabrina's Mum was right about one thing, I thought, while unlocking the cottage door; Little Miss Perfect did make the front pages after all.

The Chimes at Midnight

High above me the Hunter's Moon cast its lengthy shadows as the first flurries of snow fell. The bitter wind tugged at my skirt as I crossed the wide expanse of lawn at the front of Crowhurst Hall. It was a journey I'd made many times before. In the past I had failed in my effort to put right a wrong that has been done. As the snow swirled around me, seeming almost to sweep me up and over the threshold of my old home, it felt different this time.

In the cold hallway I stood dressed in what had once been my finery, before the old long-case clock. I studied its delicate, ornate hands.

In the past, as a child, I'd found them fascinating too, but then they marked the passing of a happier time. Now I watched the seconds tick away and waited for its hourly chimes, they did not come. Instead, they evoked some half-remembered remark in which I recalled, that the past and the present like the sweeping hands of a clock, run together.

Yet to me it seemed like only yesterday when I heard it ring out its melancholy chimes to mark my passing. They resonated around my ice-cold body before the soil fell clattering upon my coffin lid as the mourners left me beneath the frosty ground.

Now the only sound I heard was the ticking of the clock. I wondered what had disturbed the tranquillity of my eternal slumber. I knew I could remain for only so long within these walls, for I was no longer welcome. He who'd robbed me of everything I held so dear would be outraged to know I've returned once more.

My faded, black taffeta skirt rustled on the flagstone floor as I moved aimlessly around. For a moment I lingered in the library. Wisps of tenebrous memories came flooding back. Suddenly I'm aware that I am not the only restless spirit in the house.

I ascended the marble staircase. I paused and rested my hand lightly on its carved banister. The gentle smiling faces of my beloved parents, with vacant, painted eyes, stared back at me. I reminisced at their untimely passing. Something cold crept across the back of my bony neck and shoulders making me shudder. I brushed my fingertips across my icy cheek longing to feel the unshed tears. I needed to cry for what had once been mine.

I entered my old dressing room. The chilling night air filled it with dampness. Prior to my death, my servant, Annie, would've made sure a welcoming fire filled it with warmth and light, but now it was as welcoming as a cold, empty grave. In the past I would've sat before the large ornate mirror, with its exquisite carvings of cherubs, love hearts and doves. I would comb my glossy, golden tresses whilst dreaming of my darling Henry's return from London.

How my heart leapt with pleasure on hearing the sound of his carriage on the cobbles outside my window! Impatient for his embrace my heart longed to hear his sweet, whispered words of love. Now seated before the mirror all I see is bone-dry, cadaverous skin stretching across my emaciated face, as I brush dirt and worms from all that remain of my hair. Has time passed me by so quickly that I'm nothing but bones?

At the sound of the door catch lifting, I dissolved into the shadows. A young woman glided into the room. Her beauty astounds me. With raven-black hair, she was clothed only in a long, white nightgown. She crossed a pool of moonlight, her feet blue with cold and headed in my direction. In her dream-like state, she seemed to be searching for something. Her movements were exaggerated as she opened and closed drawers and cupboard doors. "How could he betray me so?" she muttered.

I stepped out of the shadows. "Hello, beautiful sleepwalker. What is it that disturbs your slumber?"

The sleepwalker's tear-stained eyes were unblinking. Yet something flickered across her forlorn face and made me realise, that unlike me, death has no claim on her. I follow her, but she shows no signs that she's conscious of me.

"Please, do not be afraid. I mean you no harm. What disturbs you so?"

She turned. Her eyes dart back and forth as though she sought a sound. I was pleased to know that she could not see me, but heard me. The sleepwalker lifted her hand to brush a strand of her raven hair from her lips.

In the moonlight I saw something shimmer. "What's this you're wearing?" I raised my bony, dust-dry hand before her face, so she saw what hung on my fleshless finger. "With this ring he did wed. So he's wed another, making us three?" My heart's broken knowing I've failed another.

Bewilderment settled on her face. Her pupils began to dilate. Then she saw me but as if in a dream. Her voice carried neither weight nor sound, like a child's sleeping breath, she asked, "Who are you?

"I'm Eleanor. Back from whence I slept so peacefully, back to warn you. Though I've failed another whom I tried to save. Fate has been so cruel."

Her brow creased as she stared right through me. Then suddenly aware I'm not a ghost, her hand flew to her mouth to stifle a cry. With trembling lips, she uttered, "Incubus! Succubus, be gone!"

In contempt I shook my shrunken head, scattering dirt, worms and hair around my bony feet. "I am neither. You may have youth and beauty on your side, but your days are numbered. As you see me standing before you, so you shall be one day. For there's no escaping from the hands of time. I wish only to see you grow old and not die before time's touch has lined your face."

Suddenly the tolling clock's mournful chimes echoed throughout the sleeping house, showing the passing of another hour.

"At last!" I cried, holding out my fleshless arms. The ravages of time were undone. I stood clothed once more, flesh upon flesh, muscle and sinew. Time restores my golden tresses, but I cannot linger. Vanity is a weakness for the living, as time is not mine.

She too awakes from her half-sleep and whispers, "You're Lady Eleanor. I've seen your portrait and your tomb in the cemetery. Five years have passed since you were murdered, by an unknown intruder, while your husband was away."

"What tale is this? Come let me show you the truth. For too soon it will become your fate, if you aren't careful."

"What truth can you show me? You were murdered!" With a shudder she hurried to her bedroom. I followed her, afraid she would wake him. In my haste I stepped into her bedroom, surprised to find how little has changed. All that we selected together for our love nest he now shares with another. The noctambulist wiped the tears from her cheeks, as she stared at her sleeping husband.

"Fear not. He sleeps on."

She glanced in my direction. Her lower lip trembled, as she whispered, "When I see him sleeping so peacefully, my heart is full of love. The way the curls of his black hair fall lightly on his ruddy cheek. See how his lips part as he breathes gently. See the line of his jaw, it is so strong. How could you not fall for such a man?"

I laughed. "Sweet night walker, if your heart is so full with love for this sleeping man, then what makes you roam alone, while he sleeps so serenely?"

A questioning look flickered across her innocent face. "Should I not fear you, Lady Eleanor? For am I not, in my disturbed sleep, talking with a ghost?"

I raise my hands to her. "I'm not here to do you harm. The living should not fear those of us who've passed over. We can do you no injury, sweet child. There's one who is living whom you need to fear far more."

"How can I trust you? You have no right to be here?"

"Let me join you in your nocturnal amble. For this was once my childhood home—"

"This much I know—"

"So what troubles you?"

She gestured to the room. "There was once another who called this house her home, but unlike you, she's not a ghost."

"Come, let's go, where we can talk more freely."

As we left her sleeping husband, he rolled over and I feel the darkness rearrange itself. I want so much for him to awake, so I can peer into his dark, soulless eyes once more, but alas, he sleeps on.

In the hallway, apart from the steady ticking of the clock, the only other sound is that of the sleepwalker's bare feet on the stone floor. As a ghost I create no lasting impression, not even sound.

On entering the library, the young woman added another log to the dying embers in the grate. With a crackle the fresh dry wood ignited, throwing its warmth and light around the room. Although its heat didn't warm my icy bones, I still shuddered as the shadows of my past gathered in every corner, waiting for me to tell my tale of betrayal.

"Please do you know about the other woman?" I feared

the worst. For I had visited her on such a night, three years ago, to warn her, the best I could, that death would be knocking at her door. Unlike this woman the second wife did not have a strong constitution. On that fateful night, before the clock struck the hour to restore me, I had stepped out of the shadows too early. She had gazed upon my worm-eaten face and her screams had woken her household.

The sleepwalker stood before the French windows, staring at the moon through the lightly falling snow. With a heavy sigh she turned. "My husband had no right to marry me when he has a wife who lives in a mental asylum. I discovered Lady Helen's journal in this very room a week ago. I read of her sadness. She haunts my thoughts and dreams. Unlike me, she was not strong and she feared destitution. Her worries slowly descended into madness, so when Henry left her alone for days to travel to London, she feared he would never return. With no money to pay the servants' wages, they deserted her. Left alone she roamed the icy corridors. Now you've appeared as if to haunt my dream – oh, why do I doubt the man I love?"

"Do you not believe her?" I heard the hesitation in her voice. "Once, she like you, believed every word he uttered. Now, I am but a ghost belonging to the borderlands. Like Lady Helen and yourself, he deceived me too. Not for love did he marry me, but for my father's money. The day he drove the knife into my beating heart he took pleasure in telling me so."

"Were you not killed by an unknown hand?"

"No. The hand that took my life was none other than that of my husband, Henry and in this very room too. He drove the knife in, while taking such delight in telling me how he'd taken my parents' lives too. He had their carriage driven off the road, after discovering my father had made inquiries in London's high society and discovered that Henry was in debt for gambling.

With my dying breath I cursed him. That's why I'm not free to sleep for eternity until he has paid his debts in full to me."

"Oh, so it's all true. He married me for my money too! While he has been away I uncovered his secrets here. When I found Lady Helen's journal and a bloodied knife, I wanted so much to believe it was not true." She crossed to a shelf, half-hidden in the shadows, pulls out the knife, and lays it before me.

"'Tis the one with which he took my life."

Suddenly, the door burst open and Henry came in. On seeing his wife seated alone, he shouted, "Oh, I do declare, my new wife betrays me not with another, but I feel madness fills the air yet again! Am I so cruelly fated to find another whom I took to be my bride is suffering from lunacy too?"

His wife turned to me and smiled.

"Dear lady, take your leave." I said. "The time has come to set us both free. Take Lady Helen's journal and keep it safe. Sleep deeply now until daybreak."

Without a word she picked up the book and took her leave.

As Henry went to follow her, the door slammed shut. He watched in horror as the key spun in the lock and then vanished.

"What trickery is this?" he cried.

Out of the shadows I appeared, still beautiful in a dark unnatural way, as I had been on the day he took my life.

"None that I can see, my Lord, but revenge for those you've betrayed with your lies." Laughing, I lift the knife, "An eye for an eye."

His eyes were wide with fear as the cold of the grave radiated from me. His face paled as he raised his trembling hands, as if to protect himself. "This cannot be. You're a ghost that I should not see. Dear God, help me and send this Devil back into the ground."

The French windows burst open as the fire went out. Shadows surrounded him as I plunged the bejewelled knife into his cold, black heart. Henry dropped to his knees. As his confused spirit began to rise, he stared down at his dying self. "What have you done to me?"

"Time to pay for your sins. Now come follow me," I turned towards the open doors.

"You cannot do this to me! I'm still breathing and can yet be saved."

With a wave of my hand he has no choice and reluctantly trails after me. We cross the lawn to the cemetery. In the freshly fallen snow only his footprints will be seen by anyone when the new day breaks.

In the distance, I heard the old hall clock ring out its melancholy chimes for the passing of the hour as the old day becomes the new. I sink into my grave, dragging down what remained of Henry's conscious self to lie at my side.

Suddenly aware of his surroundings, Henry turned to face me, just as the worms slither back into my eye sockets, nostrils, mouth, and hair, as time takes back what it had restored to me. His scream filled our narrow space.

"Oh, such joys at last to have you here beside me in this cold ground, dearest Henry. Did you think you could escape our wedding vows? Let no man put asunder, not even death could keep us apart."

As I slip peacefully into eternal sleep with my husband at my side, the gravestone above our head now told the truth: *an unknown intruder murdered us who lie beneath this cold, cold ground.*

141

The Gardener

I was busy in the garden when the phone rang yet again. I was beginning to despise the bloody thing. It had been ringing non-stop. Worse than nosy neighbours, I can tell you. Bloody reporters wanted to know everything! How they got my number? I would never know.

I stormed into the house, snatched it up, ready to give them a piece of my mind, when the voice on the other end carried me back to when I was sixteen going on seventeen.

"Hello… is that Jennifer Underwood?"

I paused, unable to speak.

"Hello, it's me," the nervous voice spluttered. "Molly… Molly Maclaren."

Suddenly I'm back in the mud-filled cemetery, under the slate-grey sky with its cutting, whistling wind. I am once more gazing into two gaping black holes where they've laid my parents to rest.

I shuddered at the memory, recalling all too clearly the loneliness I'd felt as the gravediggers shovelled in piles of mud as swiftly as they could. I looked up at the black threatening rain clouds as the stones rattled against the coffin lids, just before the heavens opened, to receive the souls of my dearly departed, while it pissed down on the rest of us. I stood shivering in the icy rain as a strange sense of foreboding washed over me. I suddenly felt that I might have been a little too hasty in what I had done.

"I'm sorry to bother you," the voice said, dragging me back to the present. "But it is Jenny? Jenny Sanders, isn't it?"

"Yes. Hello Molly. It's been such a long time. How are you?" I heard the child that I never was in the tone of my voice. A persona I've carried with me since discovering that plants like me have a darker side too.

My parents were a great deal older than the parents of my classmates. As a child you don't see your differences until someone else points them out to you, which is what my contemporaries took pleasure in doing.

No amount of arguing with them could persuade them that they were wrong in their spiteful remarks. The old man who collected me at home time *was* my father.

I can still hear their name-calling. "Mousy Jenny, mousy Jenny! Grey hair, grey eyes, old and grey before your time... ha, ha, ha! Too grey for your parents, they dumped you on your grandparents... ha, ha, ha!"

So I gave up, but not before giving them a taste of my special medicine. I added a few drops to the fruit punch bowl at the school Christmas party. It was just enough to make them vomit over their pretty, party frocks.

Once I accepted I was different, it was easier. I enjoyed being a loner far more than by trying to conform. To me their boring fathers were stupid just like their dumb pen-pushing jobs. My father was far more fascinating, for he was a botanist. Plants were my parents' life. What father didn't know about them wasn't worth knowing.

As a child I spent many a long hour listening to him as he imparted his knowledge to me. He taught me more than just the common and the Latin names for every plant in our garden. He explained the differences between medicinal plants and harmful ones.

"A garden isn't a natural habitat for plants, my little Princess," he used to say. "It's man-made, meaning many of the plants in an English garden have come from somewhere else."

This simple fact sparked a deep fascination in me to find

out more. I didn't just want to know how to grow them, but their history too. Men have fought and died over plants. During the 1500s a single bulb of a humble tulip caused a war as men's passions raged, trying to obtain one of these valuable plants.

Throughout the Victorian era the British became great plant hunters as they built up their collections, changing our landscape forever. Plants are so much more than most people realise. To some the unassuming plants like a Buttercup, Ox-eye Daisy, or Rosebay Willow herb are just weeds.

However, to others, mere weeds can be a thing of beauty. A vase of flowers on a sideboard, or even for their healing properties, but what most people don't understand is how powerful these plants can be. That's what captivated me the most – their hidden darker side.

I would like to be able to tell you what happened to my parents was a distressing accident, but fortunately for me, it turned out only to look like one. Being an only child has many advantages especially when one is young. Not having to share your parents' love and attention is very rewarding. Until their health goes into decline, then you discover you have to pay it back tenfold, especially when you're the only child of elderly parents, then that time is sooner rather than later.

I wanted to be a botanist, like my father and travel the world studying plants, but I had to forego my plans when my mother became ill. Well, not ill as such, but more of a liability. Although Mother loved gardening, she wasn't as passionate about it as my father. After years of her self-sacrifice supporting him in his chosen career, now her health was failing and she wanted them to do more things as a couple. Like coach trips to places she wanted to see, but all her whining did was drive Father into the potting shed, leaving me to see to her needs.

In Mother's eyes I was more than capable of looking after the three of us. Ever since I was little she had been fond of saying, "Jenny you have an old head on young shoulders."

When my parents fell ill I became their nurse. Throughout the day I gave them plenty of fluids and some weak, watery soup I made following a recipe I'd found in my father's notebook. Fortunately, for me, all the plants I needed grew in our garden.

I wouldn't have called Molly Maclaren a nosy neighbour, just more of an annoying one. She was one of those people who had a sense of duty. It was as though her reason for existing was to look after others, even though they neither wanted, nor needed it.

I couldn't understand why Molly and my mother were friends. The only thing they had in common was that they had lived next door to each other before I was born. Molly was a good twenty years younger than my parents. She was a tall, elegant woman with a bright smile, perfect teeth, and clear skin and always immaculately dressed in comparison to my mother, an untidy woman with no dress sense, who was terrible at keeping house.

When I was about three, my father started giving weekend lecture tours on *The Healing Properties of Plants* so I was left behind at home often to be looked after by Molly. I never saw Molly as a replacement mother, though I knew she saw me as the child she never had.

During my parents' illness, Molly was constantly popping in to see how I was coping. One evening she burst into the kitchen via the back door without even knocking.

"What on earth is that strange smell, Jenny?" Molly asked, covering her mouth with her hand.

"Goodness me, Molly, you made me jump. Couldn't

you have knocked?" I quickly doused the saucepan I had been using with a jet of hot water.

"Your Mum never said I had to." She placed the basket of fruit she had been carrying on the table, before opening a window. "Whatever that stink is, it doesn't smell right."

"Oh, that's one of Father's medicinal recipes." I smiled.

"Well, I would've thought the smell alone would kill them. It's awful," she said, rubbing under her nose with the side of her finger. "How are they doing anyway?"

"Fine, I think, though I'm a little worried. Could you check on them and tell me what you think." I emptied the last of the soup down the sink and added some bleach to get rid of the smell.

"Okay." She headed for the stairs. Moments later, she returned, her face pale. "Call the doctor, Jenny! I don't like the look of them. Something's not right."

Molly stayed with me while we waited for the doctor. When he finally arrived, he told me there was a lot of it about, but because of their age, he wanted to be on the safe side, and so he admitted them to hospital straight away.

Within a week of falling ill, my dear parents passed away within a couple of days of each other. At their inquest, the hospital consultant, a kind and gentle man, explained that because of the flu bug, which had weakened their immune system, plus their age, they were unable to fight off the infection. This, together with the toxins in the contaminated food we'd consumed the night before they fell ill, had brought about their premature death. If they survived I would've had to spend the rest of my life nursing them.

He said I was lucky not to have gone the same way as them, but being so young had helped me to survive. The loss of one's parents at such a young age is shocking, I know, but that wasn't the worst of it.

146

It was only after my parents' obituary appeared in our local paper that I found out the truth about our home. An unexpected visit from its actual owner landed on my doorstep. I never knew why my parents hadn't seen fit to tell me something as important as the fact that we didn't own our home.

Our house had once belonged to Arthur Kingsmore, a friend of my father. When Arthur had passed away the previous year, his son, Bert, inherited it. The lease on the property had ended with the death of my parents.

Short, fat Bert stood on the doorstep taking the greatest of pleasure in explaining, "You've two weeks to leave my house after your parents' funeral, unless you can find the money to buy it."

I knew I didn't have the sort of money he was looking for, so I began to sob. Through my eyelashes I saw that no amount of crying would melt his hard heart, though in all honesty my tears were more out of frustration than anything else.

Suddenly it began to dawn on me the fruitlessness of what I had done. All of my parents' careful planning and Dad's planting had gone to waste. It wasn't as though I could just dig the garden up and move it somewhere else overnight. I cannot begin to say how angry I felt. Devastated beyond words wasn't even enough.

As the dreadful man climbed into his car, I picked up the phone and made an anonymous call to our local newspaper.

"News Desk," a cheerful voice on the other end of the phone said, "How can I help you?"

"Er, I've a rather interesting life story you might like to check out, but I need to do it anonymously." I stared out at my wonderful collection of plants, hoping I could buy myself some time in which to save the garden.

After putting the phone down, tears began to roll down my cheeks. I inhaled deeply and wiped them away. "Just get digging," I told myself. "This isn't the time to feel sorry for what you've done."

On the morning of my parents' funeral I bent to gather up more unwanted sympathy cards and caught sight of the headline emblazoned across the front of the newspaper.

**TRAGIC YOUNG GIRL MADE ORPHAN
NOW HOMELESS**

In the kitchen I dumped the unopened cards onto the work surface along with the rest, before sitting at the breakfast bar to read the article.

Bert Kingsmore told our reporter that his solicitor was busy drawing up a contract to allow Miss Sanders more time to find alternative accommodation, so he couldn't comment further on the misunderstanding.

A wave of satisfaction washed over me as I grinned to myself and switched on the kettle. I sat with my head bent, trying to appear meek, rather than how I really felt… bored, during the tedious service arranged by Molly. From all around I could hear the gentle mutterings from the other mourners. Their concerns and worries drifted over to me as I felt Molly's thin hand patting my arm in a motherly, comforting way. How I wished with all my heart it was over, so everyone would just piss off and leave me alone.

As my parents' coffins were lowered slowly into the cold, wet ground a bitter wind whistled around us. I stared up at the slate-grey sky overhead. My thoughts weren't for my parents but for myself. Where was I going to live and how could I rescue all my important plants?

"I read about your plight in the paper this morning, Jenny," a voice said, behind me. As the rain cascaded down on us, I turned to see who had spoken and caught sight of all the other mourners dashing for their cars. The voice belonged to one of my neighbours, who now held an umbrella over me, as the rain ran in rivulets down my face, chilling my cheeks and soaking through my black jacket and skirt.

"Why thank you kindly, Mr Hampden." I smiled up at a tall, rather good-looking widower who lived on our corner.

"Are you here in your car?" he asked, as brightly as one could at a funeral.

I lowered my head to hide my pleasure, as an idea began to form. "Mr and Mrs Maclaren brought me in their car." I thanked the rain as I dabbed at my eyes, while trying to muster up some real tears.

"Then, my dear, as I'll be attending your parents' wake, we shall travel back in mine."

After he closed the passenger door for me, I watched through the windscreen as he dashed, umbrella held aloft, across to where Molly was just getting into her husband's car. He spoke briefly to her. She turned and gave me a quick wave.

After Molly helped me to clear away the last of the plates, along with a few straggling mourners, whom I had finally convinced that I was more than capable of looking after myself, the day from hell, as far as I was concerned, was at last over. I really didn't feel up to celebrating my seventeenth birthday, which was just around the corner, though I did hope for some good news from my solicitor, Mister Jarrold, sometime during the next week. While I waited I worked tirelessly to pot up as many plants as I could into an array of plastic containers I had to hand.

Three days later I was still busy in the garden when Mister Jarrold's call came through on my birthday. I dashed to the greenhouse quickly shedding my dirty gardening gloves and snatched up the phone from where I had left it. I tried not to allow my voice to give away my enthusiasm whilst listening carefully as he waffled on about his costs and those of the funeral, when he suddenly dropped a bombshell.

I felt my fervour waning as he explained about a clause in the original lease on the property which stated my parents were responsible for the maintenance on the house. Through my parents' neglect I now found myself footing the bill for the repairs needed on the house. I learnt that my parents' love for their garden had been far greater than their love for me. I realised in some small way maybe my mother had been right to complain as she did about my father. He had ignored what was important and buried his head in the compost heap. Now I had to forgo owning a house with a large garden, because what was left of my inheritance would be spent on repairs to the house all for someone else's benefit.

"My dear child," Mister Jarrold said. "With such a small amount of money left to you my advice would be to get a job."

I politely said goodbye, but slammed the wretched phone down in frustration. A job! Any job would do, just something to bring in the money, he had informed me. No doubt he took more money for that piece of advice.

As soon as it was light outside I skipped breakfast and set to work potting up my most valuable plants. Without stopping for lunch I worked into the afternoon. So engrossed in what I was doing I wasn't aware of anything, until an uneasy feeling crept over me. I leapt up, swung round trowel in hand. Mr Hampden stood there.

"I'm so sorry to startle you. I did call out, but you were so lost in what you were doing,"

I smiled and lowered my trowel.

"I'm pleased to know you weren't planning to use it on me, Jenny." He gave a nervous cough. "I came to ask you a question."

I brushed my hair away from my eyes. The thumb of my muddy glove caught my cheek. In an effort to wipe the dirt away I wasn't sure whether I was making matters worse or not.

"Here let me." He took a handkerchief from his pocket and stroked my cheek. "Hmm, I wanted to ask you if you've found somewhere to live yet."

I stepped away from him. "Would you like come in? I can put the kettle on. I could do with a drink myself."

Mr Hampden nodded as he tucked his handkerchief back into his pocket.

I wasn't sure what he was planning to say to me. I didn't want to look too keen. In the warm kitchen as the kettle boiled, Mr Hampden sat, whilst discreetly looking around. The kitchen that Molly had cleaned until it shone for the wake was now dusty and dirt-splattered as rows of potted plants littered all of the surfaces.

"Sorry about the mess. I just don't want to leave any of my plants behind." I lowered my head and added tearfully, "they're all I have left of my parents. I must sell everything to cover my bills. It's awful to find oneself homeless, and to lose the garden too."

I felt his strong arms encircle me.

"My poor child, dear girl," he whispered into my hair. "I hope you don't mind me saying…" he paused.

151

I leant into his chest, hoping it would spur him on. He coughed and distanced himself. Embarrassed, I turned away, adding coffee to the cups and sugar to mine before turning back to him.

"Do you take sugar?" I wiped my eyes with the side of my hand.

He drew in a deep breath. "Jenny, I know I'm a great deal older than you—" His words came out in a flurry. "You can say no, if you are shocked by what I'm about to suggest, but I've spoken to Molly... and some of your parents' other friends, and—"

I narrowed my eyes, as I turned my back to add the boiling water to the coffee while trying to calm myself. "About what?"

"Come to live with me, Jenny. I've that large house and garden all to myself. It would be ideal. You, of course, would have your own suite. You don't even have to cook for me as I'm quite capable of looking after myself. Even if it's only for a short while until you can find somewhere more suitable."

I turned to face him. "One sugar or two, Mr Hampden?"

"Please do call me Henry. One sugar, please. So what do you think?"

With my plants settled into their containers, dotted around Henry's large garden, in places I knew were most agreeable for them, I adjusted to my new life. I sold everything belonging to my parents only keeping my personal belongings, such as a few photographs, my father's old desk, his invaluable notebooks and an array of old gardening books I had collected since a child.

With no worries about household bills, rent, or even food bills, I knew I should've felt contented. Henry had even provided me with a small allowance, so even my meagre savings were happily growing along with my plants, but still there was a nagging feeling of restlessness within me.

A year after I had moved in, my suspicions proved correct. One evening after dinner Henry asked me to marry him. At forty-two he was still strikingly good-looking, with a thick head of red hair and a trim body. Henry kept fit by running every day. I agreed, deciding it would provide me more security.

After a very showy wedding, with all the neighbours in attendance, my life settled down and I began to enjoy my plants once again. Then the following spring early one morning as the sun broke through the gap in the curtain, I rose and quickly dressed, heading for the greenhouse. I was eager to get started on sowing seeds. In the warmth of the sunshine I was happily potting some passionflower seedlings and enjoying the peacefulness, when my solitude was shattered.

"There you are, Jenny," Henry said, suddenly appearing in the doorway, both blocking out the sunshine and crowding my space.

I smiled, even though a nagging feeling slithered from the pit of my stomach. I held my breath, knowing what he was about to ask me.

He stepped in and slipped his arm around my waist. "You were up early, my dear."

"I'm sorry I disturbed you, Henry, but I didn't want to waste such a beautiful morning." I focused on adding another seedling to a fresh pot of compost.

"What are those?"

"These? Oh, they're passionflowers."

"Hmm," he whispered in my ear. "Passionflower. Oh how I wish you felt as passionately about me as you do about your garden." He turned me around and took the pot from my hand. As he set it down, it promptly toppled over.

I went to reach for it, but he stopped me, pulling me into him. I felt his hardness against me, and my first instinct was to push him away.

"Jenny," he whispered. His breath coming in short sharp pants, like a dog on heat. "I've been very patient with you. But I think now is the time for us to start a family."

I looked down at the seedling lying neglected in the warmth of the sun, wanting so much to stop its delicate roots from drying out. I looked up into Henry's blue eyes and smiled innocently.

"If you make a start on the breakfast, dear husband, I shall be in soon and we'll talk about it. First, I must finish potting these up."

He kissed me. "We shall do more than just talk, Jenny." On stepping out of the green house, he said, "Oh, how wonderful it'll be to see little ones enjoying your garden."

I tried to keep a smile on my tight lips. "Maybe I can teach them all about growing plants in the same way as my father taught me?"

"You'll make a terrific mother, Jenny and teacher too." Henry's smile faded as a scowl shadowed his face. "Why haven't you planted your collection and got rid of those horrid plastic containers?"

"Oh, because they don't like having their roots disturbed," I gritted my teeth, turning back to my seedlings, tenderly gathering them up.

Death is a funny thing, unlike love; one is so unprepared for it. Within a month of our chat about starting a family, Henry became unwell. At night he became so restless that for me to get any sleep he decided it would be best for us both if he moved into the guest bedroom. Some mornings he was so weak after vomiting through the night he couldn't get out of bed for work, let alone go for his usual run.

As I entered his bedroom he turned his face towards me. Gone were his handsome features, instead a pale, gaunt face stared up at me from the white linen sheets. Black smudges under each bloodshot eye only seemed to emphasize the hollowness of his cheeks, and his once full lips had shrunken to thin, grey lines.

He tried to smile. "Jenny, your father's concoction isn't helping." His voice seemed to come from afar. On seeing the bowl I had brought him he shook his head. "I need a doctor, please."

"Hush now, you know what they say, the worse it tastes the better it is for you."

"No more, please. Get a doctor."

"I'll tell you what, if you are no better by the end of today, I'll call the doctor. Now drink up," I held the spoon to his parched lips.

"Promise me, please—" he said, unable to keep his eyes open.

"This all started because you wanted a family, Henry. Maybe we've been trying too hard in the bedroom," I laughed, wiping the spittle from his mouth.

He tried to laugh, but it came out as a weak croak. He struggled to pull himself up. His eyes widened and he began to cough violently, retching as his thin frame shook. Henry vomited up evil smelling greenish-brown bile into a bowl, before throwing himself back onto his pillow.

"Please... a doctor, Jenny."

Molly dropped in unexpectedly. On seeing poor Henry she insisted on called the doctor, who demanded we should call for an ambulance. Henry was taken into hospital for tests. A fortnight later he was well enough to return home. I began to worry when Henry's doctor requested that he return to hospital for further tests. After six weeks they allowed me to bring him home as his health had begun to improve. Henry was happy to be at home again, but unfortunately, six months later, he slipped peacefully away while Molly was on a world cruise.

At his funeral, Molly sat holding my hand again, but this time I kept the church service short.

"I just can't understand it," she said at the wake. "Henry was so health conscious. Always running to keep trim and into wholesome eating. Well, it just goes to show it isn't good for you. My Harold even said when Henry married you maybe he should've taken up running if it meant he could catch a pretty, young thing like you."

I lowered my head and started to sob, rubbing at my eyes. "Oh Henry, what am I to do without you…?"

"Oh, I'm so sorry, Jen. Me and my big mouth. You poor child, all alone again."

Sweet Henry left me far better off than my parents had, but still I had to move on. I grew to despise my interfering neighbours. Of course they all hoped that Henry had seeded his own little garden.

Forewarned is forearmed, as they say. I'd overheard Molly chatting with Harold on our wedding day. Henry had said, he hoped when the time was right, we would have the family he had always wished for and which his first wife could never provide. I took no chances, making sure there would never be the patter of tiny feet.

As the gossip became unbearable I decided I needed to escape and put the house up for sale. Lucky for me I had learned my lesson. Although a container garden wasn't ideal, it was far easier to move.

At twenty-two I found out that money doesn't last forever. Well, it seemed such a waste of my life having to work when I could enjoy having someone to look after me. I decided it might be fun to do a little travelling, so I opted to visit some of the countries my favourite plants came from, before settling down to work on a garden of my own.

I had answered an online ad. asking for a gardening companion and so I moved into an annex of a house where another avid gardener lived. My mobile garden intrigued middle-aged petite Jill, who agreed to look after my plants while I did a spot of travelling in exchange for me looking after her house and garden while she went away visiting family and friends around the world.

I know I should've invested my money in buying a house with a garden instead of renting, but if I hadn't taken the opportunity to travel when I did, I would never have met James Welland.

Some would say our chance meeting was romantic, but I had spotted him earlier while waiting in the boarding lounge. Not quite as good-looking as Henry, but James reminded me of an orchid, his presence both exotic and glamorous. Before the plane landed at our destination we were chatting like old friends and I knew all I needed to know. Single, wealthy with no children, owned a large house with a huge garden; even though he didn't garden himself he loved flowers. I've always believed it doesn't do to have a partner be as passionate about the same interests as yourself, but interested just enough not to become bored by your passion for it.

Soon after we met, James asked me to marry him. Of course my answer was 'yes'. We kept it a simple affair with just my housemate, Jill Price and James' housekeeper, Mary and her husband Roger, his driver, as our witnesses. I instantly fell in love with James' house and garden. The garden had sweeping lawns, wisteria walkways, ponds and waterfalls. At the back of the house, large French windows opened onto a patio that took me to hidden arbours and behind red brick walls and hedges I found secret gardens.

As I followed a path I never knew what I would stumble over next in this gardener's paradise.

When my travelling garden arrived, James insisted I cover the plastic pots with wonderful pottery containers if I wasn't going to plant them. I would have been happy to plant my mobile garden, but a nagging feeling at the back of my head told me everything was a little too prefect to let my garden take root yet. I fell in love with James' large heated greenhouse and couldn't wait to sow seeds in it.

In the evenings, while my new husband studied his *Financial Times,* I enjoyed surfing the internet to find exotic plants I could now grow. My father's notebooks helped me locate the exact ones I wanted. One evening I found James watching me over the top of his newspaper. He gave me such a sweet smile. "Have you found what you're looking for?" he asked.

"I think so," I grinned back. "I can't wait to see if I can grow them."

"I'm such a lucky man. Most women wouldn't get that excited unless you were showering them with diamonds and pearls."

I laughed. "Those things don't grow, so they don't interest me."

"You, my darling, are the most unassuming woman I have ever met. Lucky for me I had the good sense to marry you." He lifted his paper and went back to reading, while I clicked the pay button for my next order of seeds.

After four wonderful years of travelling and adding to my collection James asked the dreaded question. One morning while we lay in bed he slipped his arm around my neck and kissed the top of my head. Playfully he ran his hand across my flat stomach and whispered, "My darling, you've made me so happy. Life has been a joy since you became my wife. My dearest, I know how much you love growing plants, so why don't we seed your garden and grow a family of our own. It will make my life complete."

My heart sank as a picture formed in my mind – my beautiful garden trampled feet, footballs and most awful of all, a toilet for dogs and cats. Wherever there are kids there are pets too. In the greenhouse I saw rows of my special seedlings wilting and dying through lack of care and attention. I smiled. "Of course, my darling, you're right, we should share our happiness."

That's the thing about life it can be such a bitch. I didn't see much point in trying to explain that I didn't want to share my life or garden with kids or pets. If James couldn't see that I was happier on my own in the greenhouse, with my plants, then he would never understand why I didn't want children. This time I took it slowly, allowing my seedlings time to establish themselves, knowing I would need them again soon.

When we arrived back from our holiday in Mexico James' health had deteriorated. At the airport James told his driver, Roger, to take him straight to his doctor.

"You'll have to take a taxi home, my darling," James said, as beads of sweat gathered on his brow. "I'm sure it isn't anything serious."

That evening, as I helped him into bed, he told me his doctor was baffled by his illness and had taken a blood sample before prescribing a course of antibiotics. "He believes I may have picked up a bug, or been bitten by some insect while we were on holiday."

The next morning after him spending most of the night in the bathroom, I suggested James might find my father's herbal soup far more helpful than his doctor's pills. The following night he slept well and in the morning he told me he felt much better.

"Your father's concoction should be bottled and sold. I feel wonderful this morning, Jen," he kissed me passionately.

While we waited for our breakfast James sat on the patio in the sunshine. I headed for the greenhouse to check all was well. James had installed an irrigation system so I wouldn't panic about my plants while we were away. I just didn't trust the young lad, Adam, who James had hired to help me in the garden to look after my delicate seedlings. Just as I checked the cold frames to see if anything had germinated while we were away, I heard a heart-chilling scream followed closely by a loud crash.

I dashed along the path to the patio and found Mary standing with her hands covering her mouth, sobbing, while all around her feet lay the broken remains of the breakfast tray. James's head hung over the side of the lounger, his eyes stared blankly at us. From the corner of his blue lips a thin dribble of black bile stained his chin and the collar of his white shirt. My attention was drawn to his hands. They lay in his lap, locked together as though in prayer. I made a mental note to write my observations down at the first opportunity.

"Oh, Mrs Welland," Mary sobbed. "He's dead, isn't he?"

"Come on," I guided her indoors. "We need to phone his doctor. I'll see if I can find Roger."

"My dear, are you all right?" She patted my arm.

I bit my bottom lip hard as if I was fighting back the tears. "It's like losing my parents all over again, Mary, but James wouldn't want me to go to pieces now. The shock might—" I broke off mid-sentence and lowered my head. I rubbed at my eyes as though to wipe away tears.

You must make the best of what life offers, so when an opportunity presented itself, I took it. I wanted to enjoy reaping the rewards of my labour. I've been lucky in life, finding the right man at the right time, but unlucky when it comes to love, why do they feel the need to procreate? I was reluctant to have to start my garden again. However, this time, James had willed everything to me, believing I was carrying the heir to his fortune.

Hindsight is a terrible thing, I realised now, and so too was my next hasty decision. I also realised that I had been played, as I made a repeat trip to our local library to hunt out another list of best-selling crime novels for my new husband. *Why me? Why not his bloody lazy daughters?*

Every time I saw their fucking car on my drive, my blood boiled. It was the same every week for two years – oh sorry, I've jumped ahead a bit, but overall there wasn't anything remarkable in how I came to be married to Andrew Picbred.

Andrew believed in supporting his local library. Whenever his little sweethearts came a-calling, I had to stop whatever I was doing and fetch his bloody books because somehow this was too difficult for them to do on their way over. If I had known he was going to be such a pain, I would've started my special treatment sooner.

Sometimes you don't see what's under your nose. Andrew was chatty, but not too pushy, a bit of a laugh really. We met online in a plants' forum and chatted amongst a small number of the group. Then I would bump into him at a number of the different flower shows I was attending.

Of course it seemed innocent enough, but I now know it was all part of his plan. Soon he started messaging me offline, asking if I was going to the next event. I looked forward to chatting with a like-minded person. On one occasion he suggested that he did the driving. I thought it would be better if I met him halfway. He persuaded me to let him stay for the night, so we could travel together to the event. Slowly, it became the odd weekend and then longer. In no time at all he had asked me to marry him. Feeling secure within my home and myself, with him practically living in the house anyway, I saw no harm in his suggestion.

On our wedding day he suddenly informed me that he had had to sell his property after his latest business venture hadn't worked out in order to clear a large debt. With hindsight, I suppose, I should've realised he had been stalking me. It wasn't until he moved in with his collection of prized tea roses all potted up in containers I realised what a fucking fool I had been!

The straw which broke the camel's back came when one day I was busy in the greenhouse and Adam came rushing to find me in a panic.

"Missus – you better come quick – I tried to stop him, but he – wouldn't listen to me," he stuttered.

"Adam, calm down. Take it slowly. What are you talking about?" I moved a tray of pots to the cold frame.

"Mister Picbred – he's digging up some of your plants – I told him he can't do that. He said it's his garden now."

I followed Adam through to a sunny spot near the patio. Some of my well-established plants lay in a heap on the patio their roots drying in the sun. I screamed as Andrew brought the spade down slicing through a monkshood. "What in the hell are you doing?"

"Planting a rose garden for myself," he discarded one of my prized plants. "I've always fancied having one. There's plenty of the garden left to allow me to have this small patch. Anyway all you're growing here is fucking weeds."

I bit my tongue and walked away. What can one say about roses other than they are nice to look at? That's when things really started to go wrong between us and everything changed. From then on, he lavished all his attention on his roses. I was left to get on with my main interest.

It was about this time when his daughters started to visit regularly. I think to save face he hadn't told them the truth about losing his business. Andrew liked to behave as though he owned everything. It was his daughters who suggested that he pursue his dream of setting up a rose growing business by planting more of them around my garden. Tina and Freda never liked me, but Andrew always insisted they would grow to love me. It was a shame because I certainly didn't love them.

When Andrew suggested we hire a cook and a cleaner, after Mary and Roger retired, I was pleased. When he wanted to hire two professional gardeners and sack Adam because he had damaged one of his precious roses, I lost my temper.

"That bloody stupid boy doesn't know what the hell he's doing. Why have you kept him on all these years?"

"Because he does what I want him to do. I've never had any problem with him. His learning problems haven't stopped him from being a hard worker and loyal too."

"He's bloody useless!"

"It's up to me who stays and who goes, not you!"

That night I heard Andrew in the bathroom being sick. In the evening he'd dined on a spicy chicken while I had opted for baked salmon and light salad. After that food didn't seem to sit well with him. The following morning nausea hit him in the early hours. He was even unable to keep my soup down. Embarrassed by what was happening to him he suggested we hire a nurse too, but I said no. I was his wife, so I would look after him. Since his illness his two darling daughters had kept away, not wanting to catch the sickness bug, or so they told me over the phone.

Every day he got weaker and paler. Soon some sort of

paralysis laid claim to most of his body confining him to a wheelchair. On his good days he would ask if I could take him to see his roses. When I did he complained I had neglected them.

Saying goodbye to Andrew came easily to me, unlike for his daughters. Not only were they angry with me for digging up his awful roses, but when they found out that they hadn't inherited anything apart from a few of their father's personal effects they even had the nerve to accuse me of killing him! I told them if they had visited him more often, they would've seen how ill he'd become.

When I met Charlie I fell in love. Don't get me wrong I use the word *love* loosely. To start with he was a lot younger than my normal choice in men. After the trouble I had had with my last husband's kids the last thing I wanted was to rush into anything. At thirty-five I wasn't getting any younger. Charlie, ten years older than I, was a self-made millionaire, with aristocratic features and no children, which made him my ideal soul mate. For the first time in my life, I wanted to settle and have a real marriage which went on forever rather than a few years.

Charlie was such fun. Business trip or not he would take me with him. Having our own jet plane meant we were free to travel anywhere; one day to Paris, then over to South America, the following day China.

I was in heaven. While Charlie was at a business meeting I hired a jeep and set off to see the plants growing in their natural surroundings. For once death was the furthest thing from my mind. One day when I came in from the garden I found Charlie in the library studying the books in my gardening section. He turned, but his smile didn't light up his mischievous brown eyes. "An interesting collection you have here." He patted the spines of the books.

I laughed. "Why thank you. I didn't know you were interested in gardening."

"We can't know everything about each other straight away otherwise the mystique would be gone." He wrapped his arms around me, smiling broadly, but his happiness didn't show in his eyes. "Let's go out tonight. Have a meal somewhere special," he said, releasing me.

"That'll be lovely and make a nice change," I replied, trying to check exactly which books he'd been interested in.

"I'm going for a shower."

"Okay."

After he had gone I studied the shelf wondering what had caught his interest. Silly I know, but I had kept a few little mementos of my dearly departed ones; just a few odd photographs of my parents, the happy grooms and notes on which flowers and plants I like best. Like most passionate gardeners I kept notes on all my plants i.e. how well they grew, if they were true to form, from cuttings or seeds and how long they took to germinate as well as their side effects.

Not long after the incident in the library things began to change between us. Suddenly Charlie took an interest in the garden and wanted to go to the Chelsea Flower show with me. At first I was excited. We stood side by side in the potting shed planting up our new seedlings together. Charlie had become enthusiastic about growing vegetables and entering them into the village summer fête.

Somehow Charlie's excitement at winning a rosette for his first attempt at growing the largest marrow in the village was infectious. Soon we were on first name terms with other local gardeners. I must admit I began to enjoy chatting with like-minded people, though I was always careful about what I said.

One morning I woke unsure of what had disturbed me. I reached for the warmth of Charlie but he was gone. The noise came again and I leapt from the bed. In the bathroom Charlie was on his knees leaning against the tiles, his face ghostly white. The room stunk of bile.

"Charlie what's happened? Why didn't you wake me?"

Before he could speak he started retching again. Once he had stopped I lifted him the best I could and managed to get him to our bed.

"I'm calling the doctor."

After the doctor left Charlie told me to stop fussing. It was nothing but a case of dodgy prawns. While he slept I went to the greenhouse to calm my nerves. I couldn't understand what was wrong with him.

Over the next few months Charlie's health declined. No matter how many tests the hospital did they just couldn't find anything wrong with him. I panicked and argued that it wasn't possible for a healthy man to decline so quickly that he needed a wheelchair, without something being seriously wrong. When Charlie took a turn for the worse I rushed him into hospital myself. I wanted to stay, but they sent me home. Alone in our big bed I sobbed my heart out. I had never loved anyone so much, even my plants begun to suffer, as I focused on him.

I had just finished washing up my breakfast things when I heard a car pull into our drive. From the kitchen window I watched two men, both police officers, get out. My heart sank. "Charlie, dear God, no!"

Without waiting I rushed to the front door.

"Jennifer Underwood?" the taller of the two men asked.

"Yes," I stepped back.

"Mrs Jennifer Underwood nee Sanders, I believe?"

"Yes. Sorry what's this about? Is my husband all right?"

"Your husband is fine, but we are arresting you for

attempted murder," he said, as the police officer snapped on the cuffs.

Me murder Charlie! After all the practice I've had you would've thought I'd have done it properly, if I were going to. Of course it all came out at the trial. Charlie's uncle had been my second husband. How amazing was that?

The day I'd walked in on him looking at my book collection had been my downfall. He'd found the photograph of his uncle in my father's notebook. Luckily for me he hadn't understood my coded notes.

Apparently there had been whispers over the years in Charlie's family. They'd never believed Uncle James had died of natural causes. Not wanting to suffer the same fate, Charlie got in first, hoping to set me up for attempted murder. He hoped my conviction would lead to his uncle's death being investigated again, but he also hoped for a settlement with my property. What a fool he must have thought I was! You see I was ahead of the game too. I found out he had lost large sums of money through bad investments and gambling.

The judge smiled at me when the court threw the case out. In fact the verdict was 'attempted suicide' as Charlie's fingerprints were all over the poisonous plant's section of my gardening book. In the end the police charged Charlie with wasting their time even though he told them about what had happened to his uncle.

We're divorced now and I even got a nice little settlement too.

"Of course, dear Molly. How are you?" I stared coldly at the phone in my hand whilst I softened my tone.

"I'm fine, Jenny. Good to hear your voice after so long."

"How's your dear husband, Harold?"

"Sadly, he's no longer with me. Passed away a few years ago."

"Oh dear. Sorry to hear that Molly. You're on your own now?"

"No, my niece Jean and her son, Tom, come to mine whenever they can. He's such a clever lad. He found your name and number on the net. I'm not au-fait with computers myself. Tom is a bit of wiz. I think he helps to track individuals down. Though he doesn't like to talk about it. Anyway, how are you?"

"Oh, so that's how you found my number. I'm sorry, Molly, but I can't chat for long. I'm on my way out." Molly's revelation had answered my question about how the reporters have found my phone number.

"Off somewhere nice, I hope?"

"Out for a meal with Samuel Fairfax, such a sweet man," I answered without thinking.

"Isn't he the judge who cleared you? I've been following your court case in the papers and on the television. Should you be seeing him?"

"There's nothing to stop us. My court case is over. Anyway he's asked for my help with a gardening problem." I stared out at my beautiful garden. "I'm sorry, Molly, I really must go. Lovely chatting to you after all these years, but his Honour doesn't like to be kept waiting. Call again soon."

I reached to switch the phone off when I heard her say, "I wouldn't rush into this one, Jenny, like you did with all the others."

I felt my heart lurch. "Sorry, what are you talking about, Molly?"

"What I said."

"If you're talking about my gardens, Molly, one must remember the saying *all good things come to those who wait.*"

She laughed nervously. "I meant where is Judge Fairfax taking you?"

"Oh – to his house. I'm helping him sort out his garden. It used to be his wife's pride and joy before she passed away.

"I see. So he's wealthy too?"

I detected the bitterness in her voice. "What on earth are you suggesting Molly?"

"Oh, you know, Jenny, what gossip is like."

Molly, you were always a nosy cow, I thought, as I watched the judge's car turn onto my drive. "I'm so sorry Molly, I have to go now. Samuel has just arrived. Are you still living at the same address?"

"Yes. I am. Do come for a visit, Jenny. It would be lovely to see you."

"Of course, I shall. We can chat about the old times." I stared out at my garden, my mind already searching for just the right plants. "I shall choose something extra special from my garden for you. Bye for now, Molly. Thank you for calling."

Rat Trap

Are you asking me if I believe in forgiveness, lady?

Ha, then you need to hear it from my point of view. In my experience, those who beg for mercy seldom deserve it.

Tonight, for some reason, sleep eluded me. In desperation for slumber I rolled onto my back hoping to snatch at least a few hours of restless sleep. That's when a door slammed, robbing me of even that much. Under normal circumstances, I sleep well, even better after the excitement of a kill. Although I've always believed that it's the smell of blood and fear that soothes my tormented soul, helping me to find rest.

For the first time in years I've been unable to find some sort of solace, even in sleep. In my frustration I gave up and switched on the light only to find my prayers had been answered. Like some half-forgotten dream I woke to find you're here. Though our time will be short, I'm sure it will be enjoyable. You can keep your bloody questions.

I've got a couple for you. First, what's wrong with the lighting in this place? You really ought to sort it out. It's far too dull.

Oh, so it's supposed to calm my nerves? Well, that's the last thing you should be concerned about – the state of my nerves.

Why are you wandering around at this ungodly hour anyway? Can't you sleep? Maybe you've something to hide too.

Ha. Are you really expecting me to believe you came here tonight because you needed to talk about my relationship with my mother? Couldn't it have waited?

Questions… more bloody questions.

As you have robbed me of my sleep, I might as well answer them. Overall, my mother was a good woman, maybe a little too bossy. No, in all honesty I've no idea how other mothers behave towards their kids.

Now look here! If you want me to answer your bloody questions, you're going to have to listen. Anyway, what gives you the right to say my isolation was the cause of my so-called problem?

I don't have a problem. All I know is Mum enjoyed living alone, especially after Dad left.

Maybe you're right. Mum opting for home schooling made things easier for me, but she was a qualified teacher. I expect it helped her too with the nearest school being many miles away. Oddly enough Mum didn't mind getting us up early every Sunday to drive to the nearest church. And no, before you ask, we weren't originally church-going folks. Only after we moved, Mum started insisting we attended. Yes, it was before Dad went.

What? You think I'm making excuses for my behaviour. Let me tell you, lady, you have it so wrong!

Mum was a proud woman and would often tell me, "We're God-fearing people, Aaron. I want everyone to know we're living the way the Good Lord expects us to live." And Lord didn't I know it. Every morning and every night she had me kneeling on the cold, stone floor, praying. Not just a quick prayer for world peace, nope, she had a long list of things we needed to pray for, including Dad. Well, he was last on the list. I did wonder whether she hoped he'd return, but I knew that was impossible.

Mum had some funny ideas about God and how 'He' worked in mysterious ways. Bless her. She was fond of telling me, "Son, no matter what you do, God forgives," as if I believed in all that shit. His infinite powers? Bollocks!

At the age of twelve I realised I wasn't like other boys. God, I could do with a drink right now! Do you want one? Ha, going by the look on your face, my secret stash has taken you by surprise. You'd be amazed how we inmates manage to get stuff brought in here.

No prison walls are too high for us. Funny that you should say I shouldn't drink. Yeah, you're right. It brings out the worst in me. Well, I guess, that's something else my mother would've agreed with you on.

"The devil's brew, that's what drink is!" It's what she used to holler at Dad, so I guess it's lucky she's not here with us now. Whiskey was my dear old dad's favourite tipple. Not that Mum would ever allow him to enjoy his in peace. Her constant nagging drove him to seek solace in the woods.

I think we should raise a glass to him, don't you? Let's hope he found the peace he craved so much. I don't enjoy drinking whiskey from a plastic beaker. I much prefer a lead crystal glass. The one thing I've learned while being in here is to make the best of what you have, while you can. So you want to know more about my home life? What so you can get inside my head, Doctor? Do you think it will make a difference to the outcome?

Okay, I suppose some might've been jealous of Mum's inheritance. A stunning house in the middle of nowhere, surrounded by trees and with a beautiful lake. I remember with perfect clarity Dad's excitement the day Mum received the keys. We wound our way along the old farm track, bumping over ruts and potholes. It seemed to go on forever. Finally, Dad brought the car to a halt beside the lake and jumped out.

"This is so stunning, Mary! I can't wait to see what fish are stocked in the lake."

Mum cut his plans short. When he climbed back into the car, Dad realised he wasn't going to live *his* dream, but instead pay for ours.

Dad began to skulk out of the house through the garden

and into the woods. Sometimes, unbeknown to him, I would follow ghost-like. It became my favourite game. I'd hide among the undergrowth, unseen and unheard. Loved seeing the look of fear on his tired face as he stumbled and staggered through the dark wood. Occasionally, he would look over his shoulder, trying to see whom or what followed him to his log cabin sanctuary. Here he had gathered our past home comforts around him.

From the day we moved in, Mum began to shed her past life and ours too. Everything that displeased her was thrown out, including Dad's battered old armchair and his collection of Zane Grey Westerns. Anything she saw as inappropriate reading material was binned.

Everything Mum discarded, Dad saved to furnish his bolt-hole. His chair took pride of place as it once had in our old home. In one corner of the hut stood an old pot belly stove in which he burnt her romantic novels and those women's magazines that no longer met with her approval. Within his cabin he read his forbidden books, while slowly getting drunk. Some nights he wouldn't even bother coming home, preferring to sleep it off and then in the early morning take a swim in the lake before returning home to eat a hearty breakfast with mum and me.

Dad soon got tired of doing nothing and became his own boss. His small income allowed him to overindulge with the bottle whenever he wanted. On Dad's good days he would encourage me to help him cut logs for our fires and to sell. My job was to chop the kindling for the kitchen stove.

I enjoyed being in the open air, when it was just Dad and me. He would watch me with such pride in his eyes, telling me what a good lad I was. In return I beamed back at him.

The smell of the wood excited me almost as much as

the weight of the axe in my hand. As for the sound of it slicing through the wood… thwack…! My mouth would go dry. Oh, the joy, the feeling of… sweet, so sweet…

No, I must keep to my story. It's important for me that I tell you it in sequence so you will fully understand. By the time my little brother, Pete, died, Mum had completely transformed herself and our world. I always believed our world was complete, perfect. *'Our perfect world'*, Mum constantly called it, while tucking me into bed when I was a small boy. *'We don't need anyone else'*. Just the three of us Me, Mum and Dad.

As I recount those days, I see some clarity in just how much was lost when we moved to that unforgiving house. Yes, unforgiving is the right word. Look lady, I don't have much time, so do you want me to tell you the rest, or shall I start now?

Okay. Dearly departed great-aunt Livinia's house was a grand Gothic affair. For centuries it had lurking within it a dark soul. Its eye-like windows had watched and waited, while life's imperfections played out within its rooms and grounds. If you thought the outside looked unwelcoming, then the inside was even more so.

Livinia adored everything morbidly depressing. Amongst her dark furniture and claustrophobic dusty furnishings was a large collection of stuffed birds and animals that stared down at you with jet-black soulless eyes. It was a taxidermist's wet dream and added to the already sombre atmosphere.

"Good God, Mary, I feel like I've come here to die. The house feels as though it will suck the life out of your bones," Dad said, as we entered the mausoleum-like home. "Well, I suppose once you've done your interior decorating magic it will feel less like our final resting place and more like heaven on earth."

Mum smiled her beautiful smile, rolled her sleeves up and started to clean the kitchen. As the days passed the house began to shine, not just with fresh paint and furniture polish, but with our happiness too. I'm not sure what caused my parents' change of heart and marked the end of my happy childhood.

After all I was more than happy to be the centre of their world. I fondly recall the closeness I shared with Dad. How he used to ruffle my hair when he found me sitting reading a comic or watching telly.

Pete's death changed Mum. She took exception to the television; hating the fact Dad spent too much time watching it.

"Can't you switch that thing off for once?" she screamed at him.

"What the hell's wrong, woman? A man's got to have some way of relaxing after a hard day's grafting."

Once Dad had left for work Mum took a hammer to the TV. As the clock ticked closer to the time Father came back from the woods, I hid in my bedroom, knowing a slanging match would begin when Dad saw what Mum had done.

I'm not sure who was to blame for what happened to me. Not knowing whether it was the way my parents treated each other, or was it the fault of the rat? What do you think? Oh, haven't I told you about the rat. Well, if you're sitting comfortably then I shall begin. Once upon a time, there was a rat... ha. That's so funny... *Are* you sitting comfortably? Guess not going by the look on your face. Sorry, unfortunately my humour is rather dark.

Anyway I was about four years old at the time. Mum was preoccupied with decorating, and Dad was out in the woods somewhere. I slipped outside and began exploring the outbuildings.

At first nothing much interested me. Then I heard a low

175

pitiful squeaking, closely followed by clunk, clunk noise in one of the buildings. Curiosity overcame my fear and I went in to investigate. In the centre of the floor sat a big, brown rat, with long yellow teeth. The sight of it startled me until I realised it was trapped. It seemed wedged by its tail between two full petrol drums, its body on one side and its tail snared in a trap on the other. I nearly wet myself laughing. It was unable go forwards or backwards. It couldn't even reach its tail to chew through it to free itself.

Can you imagine making a choice like that? Deciding whether to chew through your own leg, or wrist to escape or die of hunger? Hmm, I quite like the idea of watching someone so desperate to make such a choice. Ha, your face, it's a real picture!

Anyway, back to the rat. I poked it with a stick. It squealed. The sound was amazing. I buzzed with energy. For once I was in control. It was a delight to watch its feeble efforts as it tried to scale the side of the drums, but the trap held it fast. Every time it stopped trying to escape and lay panting, I poked it again. This sent the rat into a snarling and squealing frenzy. I looked around for something better to poke it with. As it kept gnawing at my stick the rat bled from its mouth. Droplets sprayed across the floor, upon the cans and soaked its fur. The rat danced about in an effort to escape as I hunted in a cupboard and found a screwdriver.

I poked the rat as hard as I could. The blade slipped sweetly into it. When I pulled the screwdriver back, a jet of hot blood showered my hands, making them sticky. The rat lay on its side twitching until it became still. Then I picked it up by the trap, carried it outside and tossed it and the screwdriver into the stream. I washed the blood off my hands and went home for dinner.

After that none of my other silly toys gave me as much pleasure as tormenting the rat had done. Hmm, it's funny looking back. I see it all in a different light, where previously it all seemed perfectly normal. Anyway, shall I go on? Okay, I'll take your nod as a sign to continue. My parents suddenly had the bright idea of getting me a doe-eyed pup. They had some romantic notion of seeing the dog and me growing up together. I had plans of my own.

Early one morning while lying in bed I tried to work out how to make the pleasure last longer than it had done with the rat. As I contemplated I recalled the sweet smell of the blood. It filled my mouth and nostrils. Don't get me wrong, I don't drink blood. That's too disgusting. It's the smell of it. You breathe it in until you can taste it on your tongue. Like the smell of fish and chips instantly makes you crazy for them.

As I recollect it took me ages to find that stupid dog after I had eaten my breakfast. It was as if the mutt knew. In the end Dad brought it to me. He laughed and said, "I don't know what's wrong with the poor little thing, I expect it's pining for you." He handed me its lead and ruffled my hair before heading indoors. Just as he got to the top step he called over his shoulder, "Have a great day, son, but don't be late home. You know how your mother worries about you."

I could see fear in that mutt's eyes as though it had read my mind. It twisted and turned on its lead wanting to strangle itself rather than let me have my fun.

Hey, lady, I can see that same look in your eyes. Don't worry; I haven't finished my story yet. What I can't understand is why my parents couldn't see that I was happy being on my own?

Anyway, things came to a head when Pete died. Mum went to pieces. I don't understand why she got so upset when she still had me.

I was six years old when it happened. Mum was busy in

the kitchen cooking. Dad lay stretched out in our parlour watching the telly. Pete started to bawl. Mum had only just fed him and put him down for his nap. She shouted to Dad to check on him.

Dad shouted something back, but Mum didn't hear. I thought I would help and crept along the hallway to his nursery. Mum regularly told me how lucky I was to have a baby brother, but I couldn't see it myself. She insisted when he was old enough I would enjoy taking him fishing. She even remarked I would never be lonely again. Loneliness wasn't something I felt. I enjoyed my own company. What fun could there be with a shitty little baby?

There was only one game I wanted to play with him: my special game. But I'd known I had to wait for the right time. As I stepped into the nursery I knew the time had come. That it was down to me to set my parents free. After all four was too many in our family. Maybe he knew too, as he started to whimper, just as the puppy had.

I wondered if he was able to read my mind. Maybe he was able to control my parents too, like when he cried for their attention. I realised then what I needed to do was stop him. His eyes seemed to follow me around the room, as though he understood clearly what I was about to do. It was as though all the wisdom in the world was born within him, but he had yet to master the language to be able to call for help.

I was disappointed. I had no fun at all. It was far too clean. I held his stupid fluffy teddy bear over his whimpering face. The one Mum had bought for me to give him on his arrival at our home. After a moment he stopped moving. I used the stool to replace the bear back on the shelf.

Of course I always put things back where I find them. Well, almost everything apart from the crying baby. I closed the door behind me and slipped back into my room. Soon Mum called us to the table. After dishing up our dinner she went to fetch Pete. Her scream still haunts me some nights, especially when I don't have a good kill.

It's the sort of scream that vibrates through your body tearing at your soul. It's as though they're in hell and there's no escape. It's as though something inside of them is dying. I covered my ears trying to shut the noise out. I couldn't understand why she was screaming. Hadn't I done just what Dad wanted Mum to do when he had told her, "Can't you shut the kid up? I'm trying to watch the telly." I was being helpful by shutting the bloody thing up for good.

The police came, then the ambulance. The house seemed to suck everyone in until it was full of people asking questions. I thought about the rat, when they carried Pete out. I became 'the poor little mite.' Everyone was extra kind to me, ruffling my hair and trying to make me smile. A nice woman kept asking questions. She wanted to know if I helped Mummy to look after the baby.

"Mummy did not like me touching the new baby. She said I played too rough, but I'm good at playing on my own."

A puzzled look crossed the lady's face and then she scribbled something in her notebook. I smiled at her and she hugged me, telling me not to worry because Pete had gone to a better place. I couldn't see it for myself but I didn't tell her as she might've got cross. Suddenly I felt uneasy and didn't want to play the game anymore.

Pete's death unhinged Mum. She blamed herself for not checking on him sooner and she had already blamed Dad for watching too much telly. She shouted at him for not spending enough time with his children. The police hadn't helped either. A child's sudden unexplained death always pointed the finger of suspicion at the parents first. They

179

began to question whether Mum was fit to look after me. That's when she started to take me to Sunday Mass.

In the church was a statue of Christ. Every Sunday he stared down at me with his arms outstretched and hands soaked in blood. Mum told me the blood signified the sins of the world but I knew it was just red paint. Though, I have to admit, I adored the statue's face, with its look of pure agony.

I saw the same look on my Dad's face as I brought the axe down… thwack… and took off his hand. From his kneeling position he crumpled, staring up at me with a shocked questioning look as though he saw someone other than me, his son, standing over him. Oh, how richly the bright red blood sparkled in the afternoon sun, flowing like the stream after heavy, summer rain. I thought of the statue with its blood-soaked hands. It's funny, how the little things stay with you, lady.

Dad's hand lay where it fell, palm up and within it a pool of blood gathered. A halo of blood edged his wedding ring making it glisten, as his life ebbed away. I was disappointed that the hand didn't lie twitching like the rat or the puppy after I ripped its throat out. I even wondered if Pete would've done the same if I had knifed him instead of using the stupid bear to smother him.

Dad moaned softly grasping his bleeding wrist and begging for mercy. I took the axe and chopped at his throat. He raised his good hand in a feeble protest, but I ignored him. The warm spray coated me and I closed my eyes as I continued hacking, enjoying the rhythm.

Once the thwacking sound stopped echoing in my ears, I stepped back to admire my handiwork. The intoxication I felt was far better than with the rat, or even the puppy. I realised I understood fully what the vicar had said at Sunday Mass about seeing the light. At ten years old I saw the light and knew it was the best game ever.

Dad always complained that I was on the scrawny side. He said chopping wood would help me grow big and strong. As I admired my handiwork I had to agree with him. He was also fond of telling me how good I was at tidying up. On seeing the mess I had made I knew it wasn't a good idea just to leave him lying about in the open. In the fading afternoon light I took the easy option rather than trying to dig a hole or drag Dad to the lake to sink him.

I was far smarter than Mohammed. Instead of going to the mountain, I decided to bring it to me. I rolled Dad up against a log pile and began to cover him with his own stock. In all of the time Dad had worked at accumulating his wood store Mum had only visited the place once. He took pride in explaining to her how he made and sold charcoal along with other by-products of wood. Mum listened with an air of disinterest. The only comment she made was that there was enough wood to last us a lifetime. In Dad's case I guess she had been right on that score.

All through the church service I enjoyed staring at the statue of Christ amidst his agony, until I became aware of Mum watching me. Her face was a picture of serenity as she smiled at me. One day I overheard her telling the priest that she thought I would join the ministry soon. She explained to him that I understood Christ's suffering. She felt that the painting of Christ in my bedroom was the catalyst that had set me on my road to Damascus. I laughed behind her back.

Oh yes the painting gave me enlightenment, especially when the moon's rays fell across the pained face of Christ. It aroused such excitement in me. At first I was too young to understand the pleasure I felt when my body reacted on seeing his pained expression, all I knew was I enjoyed it.

Of course Mum had to go. She became a little tiresome. A few days after Dad had abandoned me in the woods one of his customers, who happened to be a police officer, discovered me wandering about dazed, dirty and soaking wet. He questioned me about why Dad had left me alone but I had learnt that being a bit vague paid off. They combed the woods and dragged the lake looking for him, but on finding no evidence, or an explanation for his disappearance, Dad became just another family deserter.

Apart from the congregation Mum didn't have any real close friends. As for me I never had any friends in the first place. Soon everyone forgot about Dad's disappearance and moved on with their lives. Now there was just the two of us. But somehow my happy home had lost its sparkle. Mum locked herself away in her bedroom for days on end leaving me to look after myself.

At twelve I had shot up in height and put on weight. Taking up running had built up my stamina too. With no parents worrying about what I was up to I began to explore the house. On discovering a large and spacious cellar I decided to check out its possibilities. Though badly lit, with just an odd dull and dusty bulb dotted about, it opened into a cavernous hole. Among the discarded broken furniture and boxes ghostly shadows moved in my torch light as I made my way between them. Deep within the cellar was a small, windowless room. I turned off my torch and stood inhaling the damp, stagnant air as my mind played out different scenarios of ways to lure Mum into this hidden room.

One thing was for sure it wouldn't be easy as she feared enclosed spaces. If I had learnt anything in my short life it was that fear and darkness are a deadly combination to most people, but to me they held my fascination.

The problem was, for me, that if there was one thing Mum feared more than the darkness, it was having no power in the house. We had no television, papers or radio, so we didn't know about the powerful storm heading our way. The first we knew was when the strong winds brought down a tree and the lights began to flicker. I was reading in my bedroom, when a knock came at my door.

"Come in."

"Aaron, what's wrong with the lights?" Mum hovered by the door her face thin and pale in the flickering light.

"I'm guessing it's just a storm, Mum. Nothing to worry about. It'll soon pass."

She stepped further in. "I wish your Dad was here." Her voice quivered as she spoke.

I looked up, stunned. It was the first time she had mentioned him since his disappearance. Mum sat on the end of my bed with her hands covering her ears, rocking backwards and forwards. Outside the wind and rain gave forth a torrent of wailing. It pounded against the house. Inside the flickering lights danced in time with the rhythm of the wind and rain.

"Isn't there anything we can do to stop the lights from flickering? It's driving me crazy."

"We could check the fuses." I closed my book.

"Oh yes, of course, the fuses. Though I'm not sure where the fuse box is?"

Neat, I thought and smiled. "In the cellar, I suppose." As the lights flickered again I slid off the bed. *How perfectly sweet this was.* Mum, dressed in jeans and a large fluffy jumper, hesitated at the top of the cellar steps. Below her the low wattage light bulbs flickered in time with the raging storm. "Do we have to go down there?" Her voice sounded like a frightened child.

"Yes, but it'll be all right. You have me. There's nothing to be afraid of."

She patted my hand. "I know I'm so lucky having you, Aaron. You've always been so strong, so self-contained, knowing just what you want."

For a moment her comment puzzled me, but her smile softened the lines around her mouth and I dismissed it. I shone my torch into the darkness as Mum followed behind. Carefully I helped her pick her way between the broken chairs and discarded boxes.

"I should've insisted your Dad cleared everything out from down here when we first moved in," she said. "There were just too many other things to do at the time."

We went deeper and the noise of the storm seemed to fade. I guided her towards the hidden room. We hadn't gone far when I suddenly sensed that she was no longer behind me. In frustration I retraced my steps and found her standing under one of the light bulbs peering into a crate.

"I wonder—?" Her voice was steady as though her fear had deserted her.

"It's not far now," I said, my excitement growing.

"We don't need to be down here, Aaron," she said, with a flat inflection that seemed to mirror her air of calmness.

"What?" The sharpness of my reply made her turn in my direction. I caught her in the torch beam. Her face, marked by age and uncertainty, seemed to take on a look of reverence. I moved around her and was delighted when the heavenly scent of fear filled my nostrils. Had it really been so long since my last kill? My hands shook at the thought of what was about to happen next.

"I remember now," she said, so softly. "It isn't down here."

"It is!" I snapped, pointing the torchlight in the direction of the small room. "It's just a bit further on." The darkness sucked at us as the next light bulb swung slightly revealing a ring of dust particles.

"No!" The single word held all her lost strength and self-belief. "It's in the kitchen."

As she pushed past me I slid the knife between her ribs.

She stumbled and put out a hand on a crate. I smiled into her puzzled face as her hand dropped to her side.

"Why?" Her voice trembled, as though some long-forgotten memory had fleetingly returned.

I thought she was asking about the knife, but then realised she wasn't.

"How did you know?" I asked, perplexed.

She looked down at her hand and I saw, within my torch light, the blood that covered it. She leant against a wooden crate. "I saw you enter your brother's room, Aaron. He was so small, so vulnerable… Why? I had enough love for both of you." She wobbled slightly, her breath coming in rapid pants. As her legs gave she slipped down the side of the box.

I laughed. "Love, Mum? It has nothing to do with '*love*', but everything to do with me doing what I wanted."

"Your… Dad?" She struggled to get the words out, but her needing to know gave her added strength.

"Him too," I said, pleased she had realised I had been capable of killing him.

"I thought so."

I leaned over her. "Why didn't you say something while you had the chance, Mum?"

When no answer came I knew she had joined the rest of my family.

Nope, I've a lot to thank my parents for. After all they created me. If it weren't for them I wouldn't have found my true path in life. Take my looks for instance. A picture of innocence, don't you think, Doctor?

I've used this face to my advantage. Women adored me. Men trusted me. In this age of enlightenment with gender-fluidity, I can be whoever I want to be, with my soft boyish looks, fair hair and skin and blue eyes. Others have found it easy to fall in love with my charms, making it effortless for me. Most people blame their mother for their own failures, not me. For me, it was one stupid rat, so bloody annoying. I had been so vigilant, never staying too long in one place, especially after a kill.

Careful in my selection I chose only the most vulnerable. Those in need of a friend or just wanting someone who cared enough to listen. I learnt that from my good friend: Jesus. Only I didn't bother with the 'do unto others as you wish done unto yourself' crap.

You'll be surprised by how many sad, lonely people you pass every day in the street. You might even work with them. Grey nondescript people who show no emotion, or enthusiasm for life, apart from complaining about it. It's only after they've experienced life from a new dimension that they get a taste for living. Then, wow, the change is amazing! They bloom like a rose in the summer rain.

When the time comes they beg like no other. Whining and crying. Suddenly they really do have something to complain about. So in answer to your question, *why kill them?* Surely now you understand? It's the reason for my existence.

I don't see why I should forgo my pleasures just because they wish to live. I invested my precious time in showing them life is worth living. If only they had put a bit of effort into seeking out enjoyment for themselves instead of just complaining, then I wouldn't have found them. That's what my motivation is all about – my enjoyment, my pleasure. Oh yes, there's been quite a few. Why does it shock you, Doctor? Haven't I just explained how easy it is to find discontented people?

No, I don't see it as being cruel. I've given them my undivided attention, creating a need, a desire in them to be loved and understood. A promise I've fulfilled. Oh yes, I've loved every one of them. In return they've added a new dimension to my game by sharing their love with me.

In some cases, it might've taken me a week, months, or even a year of careful planning to set the scene for my game of make-believe. Don't think I don't have any remorse for what I've done. I assure you I do. I've found it draining and time consuming being so careful. It takes more time preparing for the moment than the length of the pleasure I receive in the end.

Constantly changing locations often made it harder to find the right place in which to create my land of make-believe. Once I've located a suitable place I then have to invest my time in staging the scene. The house has to become a home filled with love for my perfect family, with photographs of Mum, Dad and me. It's surprising how many people regret not having a perfect childhood like mine. I'm able to win their trust so easily, because of my happy tales about my loving family.

Once their happiness grows, chasing away their sad, grey faces forever, so they become a portrait of life itself, that's when my excitement reaches its climax. Just like God, I snatch it away by slipping my hands around their throat. I love seeing their startled eyes as they realise the end has come. Thank God I gave up on the axe. It's far too messy. Like a cat with a mouse I enjoy playing with them. Oh, the needle game, one by one is so much more fun.

It's funny that tonight of all nights you should arrive here with your questions, Doctor. I've been so restless lately wanting to play my game just once more. To feel that heightened excitement that I've shared with all I've ever loved. If only the police hadn't taken my phone away we could've shared my fond memories together. I'm certain the police have viewed them already. Still seeing you tied up reminds me of my final pleasure. Unlike you she was calm and didn't gnaw at the ropes that bound her wrists. She seemed resigned to the fact she would die. You're not the only one who thought I wasn't aware that every time I turned my back they would try to loosen the ropes. Don't be surprised. That's what enhances my game. Your helplessness ignites your desperation and that's what triggers your fight or flight survival mode. To me it's like revisiting the trapped rat of my childhood with the added buzz of being in control of someone's life and ultimately their death.

Out of all those I've loved, both men and women, the final one was the strongest. She didn't beg. Those who do, in my experience, seldom deserve mercy. Her silence added another dimension to my game. After weeks of indulging her it was time for my pleasure. I understood her confusion. I had seen it in others before.

Within the dark basement amongst my landlady's discarded rubbish, my Sleeping Beauty awoke into a shadowy world. Day after day I waited to see fear within Beauty's eyes, but it never came. Then one day, while she watched me with her knowing eyes, a rat appeared from beneath an old Gothic-style ornate wardrobe that stood in the corner of the basement. Briefly I stood transfixed, doubting what I saw. Its shiny beady eyes locked onto mine. It sniffed the air as though it could already smell blood, before disappearing from whence it came. My Beauty must have seen the bloody rat before I did.

At twenty-six-years-old I wondered whether I was losing my touch. Had I become too cocky? I dismissed the rat and continued with what I was doing. As I reached for the second needle the wardrobe door burst open. The bloody rat had brought her freedom along with the police.

The pest-controller had broken through from the neighbour's cellar and found her locked in mine. She had been far cleverer than I had realised biding her time and mine too. I even wondered if she knew there was a doorway hidden within the old wardrobe.

I know you're hoping for the same by keeping me talking. I wouldn't want you to miss out on experiencing my game for yourself. After all isn't that why you're here so late at night with your bloody questions? Let's be less formal, Doctor Newton. May I call you, Jill? I'm only sorry that you can't enjoy the full experience. I hope the strips of sheets aren't too tight? But at least we can have some fun.

As her eyes widen with fear, I slip the first needle in under her fingernail. She closes her eyes and clenches her teeth trying not to scream. Unbeknown to her, it's her determination that excites me. I briefly wonder just how long it will take before she starts begging for mercy as I slip in the second needle.

Outside I hear the prison wardens banging, but I focus on my game, enjoying the last chance I had. No rats to spoil my fun this time.

Roofscapes

On the side of the Gothic building, I stand within a recess that once housed a stone-faced angel. Emotionally paralysed, I'm frozen in time. Before me, on the billboard, an old poster flutters. Torn and tattered by wind and rain it announces to the world there were nine of us. Now a new advertisement, partially covering the old poster, states that the exhibition contains ten sensational works of art.

Six months ago I worked, with my friend Jude, as a picture hanger in the fashionable Kasmin Art Gallery in London. To some, I was the quieter one. Naturally shy I guarded my expressions by allowing my shoulder-length brown hair to fall forward so I could avoid making eye contact, though when needed, I could be forthright. Jude was the complete opposite. Out-going, with fiery red-cropped hair, a romantic nature, and bubbly personality. Sometimes she could be a little naïve, too.

When it came to our job, we both took it seriously. Outspoken in our own opinions on what we liked and disliked. Jude always said that one day my frankness would get me into trouble, but invariably I laughed it off.

One morning when we arrived at work the manager called us into his office. He informed us that the trendsetting artist James Ravencroft would be launching his career at the gallery and we would be expected to help at the evening event.

On the evening of the event we were required to wear some outrageous, statement uniform that made us look like a pair of hookers. We stood self-consciously at the gallery entrance, handing out glasses of cheap wine to welcome the influential aesthetes of the contemporary art world to Ravencroft's swanky début exhibition.

By the end of the event when the connoisseurs raised a

glass to toast Ravencroft's achievement, Jude and I were having our own celebrations. In the ladies' loos, we stripped off the ghastly outfits and changed back into our own clothes. After Jude reapplied her more subtle shade of make-up, she turned from the mirror, and raised a glass.

"Cheers, Tina," she giggled. "Here's to the last we'll see of Ravencroft's creepy exhibition and especially him. Let's go to a bar where there's lively music so we can party until dawn."

I declined Jude's offer to join her and the rest of our colleagues for a drink. Too stressed out by the evening's event, I was desperate to get home so I agreed to lock up.

I watched them bustle away arm in arm, their laughter floating back to me. I slipped the gallery key into my pocket as my thoughts returned to the dreadful paintings. Early tomorrow morning we would send them off to their new owners. I hurried the best I could in my ankle-breaking shoes along the empty street, with its smell of traffic fumes and takeaways towards the bus stop on the corner. Relief washed over me as the bus came into view, but then without warning invisible fingers crawled across my bare neck causing the darkness to close in on me. On waking, I found I had become part of an unknown cityscape within a Ravencroft painting.

First I need to explain something of what came before so that everything will make some sort of sense. No one could describe Jude and me as professional art critics, but in the course of our job as picture hangers we had to work out how best to exhibit the paintings. We would discuss our thoughts and opinions on what the artist's work was saying to us. Unknown to most viewers there's an art to showing art, a scientific way of guiding the viewer around the exhibition. Our job is to show each piece as a single entity allowing every painting to reach its full potential.

Six months ago Ravencroft's art arrived in our gallery. Jude fell completely in love with his work, though I found the nine paintings the artist had titled '**Roofscapes**' somewhat bizarre.

Each painting was funereal to my mind. They depicted a sombre city roofscape that went unnoticed by the public as they hurried about their business. I tried to get inside the artist's mind as Jude and I hung them.

"Don't you just love them, Tina?" Jude held one end of a massive frame, while standing on the top of a ladder. "Don't you think they possess a kind of dark beauty?"

I nodded trying to stay balanced at the top of the ladder. Once I had secured my end of the painting, I stepped down. I did have to agree with Jude, there was a kind of beauty to the paintings. It lay in the artist's brushwork. He revealed to the viewer a secret panorama above the streets. The rain-washed grey slate roofs interspersed with blood-red tiled roofs, ornate stone work of angels, gargoyles, and demonic creatures that inhabited a world above our heads.

At the centre of Ravencroft's paintings, he had depicted realistic angel-type figures. I found the subject matter unnerving. It verged on torturous. Their beautiful faces showed pained expressions as though they suffered in silence.

"Why only nine?" I moved the ladder into position ready for the next painting. "It makes no sense at all and makes the exhibition uneven."

"You and your sense of balance." Jude gave an exaggerated tut and rolled her eyes as she repositioned her ladder further along.

"One needs a natural flow, otherwise it messes everything up." I attached the next large canvas to the ceiling pulleys and climbed the ladder again. I hauled the painting up. "Remember everything has to have balance, Yin and

Yang." I gave the painting a gentle nudge to swing it towards Jude's outstretched hands. "Night is to day as happiness is to sadness. It's like good and evil."

"Rubbish!" A man's voice boomed.

I gasped and let go of the pulley rope causing my end of the work of art to drop, which left me tottering on the top of the ladder. The sudden shift in the painting's weight caused Jude to lose her balance. Left clinging to the top of her ladder, Jude tried not to drop her end of the painting, too.

"Hey, be careful with that!" The man stepped forward, lifted up the dangling picture and hung it dead straight. He turned his dark blue eyes on me, his shoulder-length black hair shone under the lights. In an upper class tone he stated, "Aesthetics, my dear woman. Art is for art's sake,"

I caught my balance and stepped off the ladder.

"Ravencroft." The man's dark eyes shone with an eerie hilarity as he offered his hand to me.

I ignored him and snatched up my clipboard hoping he would just leave us to do our job.

"I love your work." Jude fluttered her eyelashes and flashed him her winning smile. He chose to ignore her and turned his attention fully on me. Ever since he had walked in with these godless pictures Jude swooned over the hedonistic, overbearing artist in his tight black jeans. I had kept my distance.

"Tina, isn't it?" He extended his hand to me again.

I nodded, still not accepting it.

He let his hand drop, unlike his smile. With a nod in the direction of his paintings he said, "You're doing a grand job, though I expect the public will find something to criticize."

"Really?" I lowered my clipboard.

"Yes… tell me honestly what you think of my work."

193

"Your work?" I shook my head. I had no wish to share my private thoughts with the likes of him.

"Yes." He blocked my way.

"I see a darkly delicious city alive in the crowded street below," Jude said.

Ravencroft turned his too sweet, too nauseating smile on her. "I wasn't asking you, my dear."

"She doesn't like your work," Jude giggled.

"I see no beauty in them," I said, forgetting myself. I glared at Jude who just shrugged her eyes still on the artist. How could she sell me out for her infatuation? After all the times I had stood by her, even lied for her.

"So tell me, Tina, what don't you like about my work?" Ravencroft ran his slender fingers through his black mane, lifting his dark locks from his shoulders.

I owed him no explanation. My job did not include pandering to the likes of him. However, he was an important client, so I reluctantly turned to the nearest painting and studied it for a moment.

In a vast, bleak landscape painted in shades of grey, dull green, blue, and inky black, a semi-naked woman stood on a stone plinth. Her arms were constrained behind her, as she leant slightly forward like a figurehead on a ship. Against the fading light of evening sky, the woman stood at the centre of the painting, surrounded by a host of saintly statues and gargoyles on the side of some Gothic building, possibly a church.

I leaned in closer to take a better look. Something about the picture unnerved me. What I'd first thought was a necklace around the woman's neck I realised was the halter-strap of a restraining bodysuit. It emphasised the shape of her breasts giving the painting an air of eroticism. It puzzled me that an artist of his reputation would have made such a blatant mistake as to illustrate the restraint that

194

held his model in situ thus giving the painting an amateurish feel.

I knew the painting was undoubtedly from his imagination. Yet, I wondered why he had deliberately painted in the halter-strap? Did he work from... still life?

Ravencroft stood directly behind me. I refused to allow him to intimidate me as his hot breath caressed my neck. I shuddered and continued to inspect the picture, trying to make sense of what it was saying to me. I focused on the woman's features. The rain had plastered her hair to her head like a skullcap. In the vast gloominess of the roofscape the only bright colour came from several small ribbons of lustrous red. I traced the ribbons that ran down her ashen face and over her hollow cheeks and I recoiled at what I saw. Four small metal bird-claw shaped clips dug into the woman's forehead and held her eyelids open. I cringed at the thought of her suffering and stepped back almost standing on Ravencroft's foot. Had he really made his model suffer for his art?

I glanced nervously over my shoulder. His pale complexion suggested that he spent many hours labouring late into the night on these paintings. He smirked at me as though reading my mind. I swallowed hard not wanting any contact with him. He bowed to me as he stepped back. I ignored his wry smile and focused on the second painting. It depicted another woman isolated in a similar position, high up on a building, but this one looked out across an alternative roofscape.

By the time I had finished examining the other seven paintings a chill had enclosed my heart. Each painting portrayed different women but in a similar sort of setting. I let my breath out slowly. Something about these stone-carved women intrigued me; they seemed so familiar. Was it an allusion to the fact that they were still living and breathing and out there somewhere waiting for rescue? As I straightened his voice filled my mind.

"What do you see, Tina?" he whispered, in a lover's tone.

Jude giggled, breaking the tension. "She's changed her mind about them. Go on, Tina, tell him."

"Are they painted from real life?" I sensed somehow that he knew what I had realised.

"Roofscapes? Yes." His eyes sparkled as his lips curled at the corners.

I looked back at the painting he had just helped us to hang – the last of the nine. I nodded in its direction and asked, "So that's painted from *your* rooftop?" I emphasised the words '*your rooftop*' though I did not know where he came from, nor did I care.

"You could say that… I paint what I see." His tone was chilling.

Jude threw him a puzzled look. She too studied the last painting and began chewing on her bottom lip. A sign, I understood clearly, that she knew something was awry. She glanced in my direction. I nodded slightly and her eyes widened.

Jude turned to Ravencroft and flashed him one of her dazzling smiles. "Well, we must get on," she said, with a sigh. "Otherwise there won't be a show tonight."

The artist gave us both a dismissive nod before leaving.

"Is there something bothering you, Tina?" Jude asked, once we were alone.

"Yes, but… Oh Jude I'm not sure you'll understand or anyone will believe me, but the women in the paintings reminds me of…" I crossed to my handbag and pulled out an old newspaper article. It listed nine missing women alongside grainy black and white photographs of them. "See for yourself."

"Why on earth do you carry this around?" Jude asked, as she unfolded the article.

"Why—? Well, you know, I've always wondered what happened to them."

Jude skimmed the article before handing it back to me. "I do remember my parents talking about them. You don't really believe that these women are one and the same?" She gestured to the huge canvas panels.

We took in the blood-stained weeping angels who stared back at us with unseeing, painted eyes. I picked up the clipboard again, flicked a few pages and studied the details for our next exhibition.

"Well… no. Let's forget about them. They're nothing more than an artist's imagination. After tomorrow they'll be gone. We'll only have beautiful, rural landscapes to concern ourselves with then."

Ravencroft stepped into a pool of light before me. The relief I felt on seeing the bus drained away. I didn't have time to scream as a numbing pain ripped through my neck. The last image I saw, as a cold mist descended, was the bus full of people passing me.

Six months after Ravencroft's first exhibition, in another art gallery, the connoisseurs gathered like laughing hyenas around a collection of ten stony-faced angels. With morbid fascination they philosophised about the artist's inspirational theme, his fine brush strokes and the significance of the bleak *Roofscapes*, but no one questioned the dark beauty of his paintings, no one but me.

I am his number ten: the ever-watchful face above the city, seeing all but saying nothing.

Acknowledgements

Thank you to my husband, Russell, for all your support and belief in me even when I failed to believe in myself. To Kathryn and my darling son Stewart, may your journey through life bring you lots of happiness.

To my two dearest friends, Joan and Ana, thank you for sharing this writing journey with me, plots and all. To Mum and Dad, thank you for giving me life. May your stars shine bright forever.

Especially for my precious grandchildren, Lilly, Logan and Scarlett, the days pass like long shadows on my heart. One day, hopefully we shall all be together again.

To Danielle, Dan, William and little Sophia thank you for brightening our days and a special big thank you to Sheila and Mike, Jackie and James, Mark and Claire, and, Rosin Stephen, Musa and Alan.

A big 'thank you' to Gill James, Debz Brown and Kim Martin for all your encouragement, words of wisdom and for the opportunity to take my first tentative steps into becoming a published writer. And a huge thanks to Aly Rhodes for helping me to knock this collection into shape.

And, for everyone else who has briefly touched upon my life. Good or bad, you've created the writer I've become.

About the Author and the Stories in this Collection

Paula R. C. Readman is married, has a son and lives in Essex with two cats called Willow and Brutus. After leaving school at sixteen with no qualifications Paula spent her working life mainly in low-paying jobs. In 1998, with no understanding of English grammar, she decided to beat her dyslexia, by setting herself a challenge to become a published author. She taught herself 'How to Write' from books which her husband, Russell, purchased from eBay. After 250 purchases he told her "just to get on with the writing."

In 2010 English Heritage published her first short story in their anthology, *Whitby Abbey-Pure Inspiration.* The following year she became the overall winner in the World Book Day short story competition run by Austin and Macauley Publishers. In 2012 she was the overall winner of the Writing Magazine/ Harrogate Crime Writing Festival Competition when the crime writer, Mark Billingham, selected her dark crime story *Roofscapes.*

Roofscapes was originally published in Writing *Magazine* and on *The Harrogate Crime Writing Festival* site. The version in this collection isn't the original story as the word count for the competition was much shorter. Paula developed the storyline and created this version to use as a prologue for her novel *Stone Angels* but she has withdrawn the prologue to create a stand-alone story for this collection.

In 2013, she had five other short stories published in anthologies. Three crime stories: *Rat Trap* by Bridge House Publishing, *Cold Calling* by Chapeltown Books, *The Gardener* by Parthian Books in their New Gothic Fiction *a Flock of Shadows* and the wildlife story *The Newcomers* by

Springbok Publications and a tale of enlightenment, *The Kite*, also by Bridge House Publishing.

Then, in 2017 Paula's work, was selected for the Waterloo Art Festival's short story competition and again in 2018. In June 2019 she started writing for an Australian publisher of horror, Black Hare Press. The company's submission call-out allowed Paula to explore her darker side.

In December 2019 Demain Publishing accepted her novella *The Funeral Birds* for publication in February 2020.

The stories in this collection follow the theme of death and loss. The story *On the Streets of Kabul* was inspired after Paula had a powerful dream, which woke her up, and she quickly scribbled it down. In the dream she was a male soldier, in Afghanistan, facing a life-threatening situation while searching for his missing comrade and childhood friend amongst the narrow alleys. *Perfect Justice* and *Shelved* were both ideas written while Paula was still working full-time in an electronics factory. The idea behind *Perfect Justice* came about after Paula's team leader at the factory, where she worked, disciplined her for making story notes during work's time. *Burning the Midnight Oil* was originally written for a competition, whose theme was to explore the many aspect of love. Paula's entry explored the relationships between family members and the choices love drives them to make.

Blog: http://paulareadman1.wordpress.com
Twitter: PaulaReadman@Darkfantasy13
Facebook: Paula.readman.1@facebook.com
Goodreads: Paula Readman
Amazon author's page: Paula R C Readman
Cafelit. co.uk Meet the author. Paula R C Readman

Other Writing by Paula R. C. Readman

The Funeral Birds
(Murder! Mystery! Mayhem! Book 3)
Published by Demain

Dave Cavendish is ready to close his detective agency for good but then Ms Sinclair swans in. Granny Wenlock knows Ms Sinclair is nothing but trouble and isn't going to allow a little thing like her death 420 years ago, stop her from warning him to be vigilant…

"*The Funeral Birds* is a fun short read that skilfully blends suspense, history, mystery and comedy as well as a touch of horror. An intriguing and satisfying story that made me want to read more about Dave, his enterprising wife, and Granny Wenlock!" (*Amazon*)

Order from Amazon:

Paperback: ISBN 979-8-634205-64-9
eBook: ASIN B084GZGRV2

Other Publications by Bridge House

Tales from Where the Wall is Cracked

by Paul Bradley

In this debut collection of short stories Paul Bradley takes a look at how extra-ordinary everyday life can be. Kitchen sink realism, magic realism and humour are deployed to present a variety of characters, many of whom live on the margins and cannot or will not fit in. In these pages you will meet a walrus man, a mynah bird called Hitler, Kendo Nagasaki, gypsy Romana, a lonely signaller and many others in an eclectic variety of edgy tales from where the wall is cracked. Wherever possible, light shines through.

"Thoroughly enjoyable from beginning to end with each story bringing the seemingly ordinary to very colourful life. Original, quirky, funny, thought provoking… and more. Definitely recommend!" (*Amazon*)

Order from Amazon:

Paperback: ISBN 978-1-907335-74-7
eBook: ISBN 978-1-907335-75-4

The Power of Love

by Phyllis J. Burton

The stories in *THE POWER OF LOVE* are quite simply about
LOVE of all kinds. If you like romance, then these short stories
are written just for you as well. There is plenty of that! The
huge clock on Waterloo station acts as catalyst for that. But the
collection also shows us other sorts of love: family ties,
enduring love, old love, forbidden love, mended love,
children's love for their parents, parents' love for their
children, a love for old buildings, and love between animals
and humans.

"If you're looking for short stories to read then look no further.
These are great reads from Phyllis. The stories are tender,
loving and well-written. I'd recommend these stories to
everyone." (*Amazon*)

Order from Amazon:

Paperback: ISBN 978-1-907335-72-3
eBook: ISBN 978-1-907335-73-0

Other Ways of Being

by Gill James

Other Ways of Being is a an anthology of stories that point us to other times, other histories, other worlds including those of our near futures, other sexualities and other genders.

Order from Amazon:

Paperback: ISBN 978-1-907335-67-9
eBook: ISBN 978-1-907335-68-6

* 9 7 8 1 9 0 7 3 3 5 8 0 8 *